Angela's Decision:

A Journey of Adaptation

gena taylor ellis

For all of those young girls who dreamed of seeing their names in Friday night lights – at the movies, on screen, behind the camera – to include my daughter…

Ursula, for the laughs, the miles and the stories shared

for Mom, a true woman of the West Virginia hills
for my sisters, cousins, aunts, grannies… daughters of the same earth
for Pat and the gift of home in Tupelo, both on screen and off
for Nancy, a toast to you and to red and white 'neath the western sky
for Bridget, and all of my fellow sisters in camo and on the home front
for all of the strong women in my life, past and present

and for Angela, my hero…

ACKNOWLEDGMENTS

Thank you to Mat King, Kate Croser, Rhiannon Owen, Xavier Samuel, Aaron Gully, and the rest of the amazing cast and crew. You breathed life into Angela and Will (Billy) on screen. You really did set the bar high in all things film for me. Thank you again, Mat. Thanks to Liam Gerner and Christopher Slaski for the beautiful music made. It stands on its own.

Thank you to my University of Oklahoma professors Andy Horton, J. Madison Davis, Joanne Rapf, Victoria Sturtevant. Thanks to the College of Liberal Studies, Sue Schofield and the MLS staff. Thanks to the Antioch Writers Workshop for that first step oh so long ago.

Thanks to Ursula for assistance in editing and for her belief in me. Thanks to some of my writer friends – Victoria for assistance and artwork for my short story, Amy and Bryan for a place at their writers' table in Huntsville, and my Oklahoma Moveable Feast mates – Maria, Ellis, John, and Rex (and one can of Spam). Thanks to my Northwestern girls, and guys, (long live Le Peep). Thanks to my film friends and film sets in Alabama and Chicago. Thanks to all of my writer and film friends and other friends I have gained along the way who inspire me daily.

And a big thank you to festival directors everywhere. You make us film kings and queens for a day. Thanks to Pat Rasberry for all things Tupelo and inspiration for putting this book together, and to Marlyn and Kat – fellow judges in arms. And a thank you to a newly-discovered festival, the Female Eye Film Festival in Toronto. You all got me back to writing again.

And thanks to all of those men and women in uniform and to their families who keep on keeping on. Always a place in my heart for you all.

Thanks to my J, to my Dad and the men who share our lives and our stories.

AUTHOR NOTES

This book contains my original short story, *Billy's Return,* the adapted screenplay, *Angela's Decision,* and an excerpt from the shooting script and the television pilot script of the same name. The award-winning film, *Angela's Decision,* directed by Mat King, is available on Amazon. I've also included an introduction before each piece. I received questions by email, from film students and film fans, after I screened the film or talked about the process of all the writings – I have tried to answer some of those here. I hope this helps in understanding the process of each one.

The fifty-minute short film is owned entirely by Mat King. I kept the rights to the story, script, and characters of *Angela's Decision,* knowing I would continue her story one day, and I have. Since it was being made as an independent film, keeping those rights was easy to do. The TV pilot script is still in competitions and has been or is still being considered by networks at this point, so only an excerpt is included here. Instead of reading the entire shooting script, you may view the film on Amazon.

Each of the pieces – the short story, the script, the pilot, and certainly the film – stands on its own. The script and film have won many awards. However, it is up to the reader/viewer to decide on the order of studying this adaptation. Some like to watch the film first, while others like to begin with the source material – *Billy's Return.* I prefer film first.

If you read the short story first, you'll know the ending of the film, and vice versa if you view the film first. Decide how you would like to be surprised, as the ending is a surprise to many, based on feedback at festivals and workshops. Enjoy reading the journey of the adaptation of *Billy's Return* into *Angela's Decision,* the story and the scripts, as well as watching the film, in whichever order you decide! It's been quite a ride.

CONTENTS

1 ON BECOMING A SCREENWRITER

Why does a pretty girl like you want to be a writer? Because I like to write.

-Frances Marion, interview with William Fox

Some women are naturals at walking in high heels, and some people are just naturals on stage. I am neither. I see no friendly faces in the audience. I see no audience. I see nothing but lights, bright lights. And I am sweating. And not the kind of sweating from running laps in physical education class or along the road down to the lake in my running shoes – some of my more natural environments.

I'm sweating as a contestant in the West Virginia Strawberry Festival Queen Pageant, which I decided to enter on a whim, along with a friend. Not the typical pageant, merely competing on looks and poise (and a who's who in town) alone, I also had to be nominated by a state representative, plus raise the funds to enter. I had nothing to lose (except maybe today's lunch), since every entrant was deemed a princess upon admission.

My sponsorship alone resembled a page out of the Yellow Pages itself, garnering more than a paragraph in the local newspaper – from a coal mining company to the local Dairy Queen to my grandmother, and plenty of businesses and relatives in between. So, that already set me apart from the other girls who were mainly sponsored by parents or just one or two local businesses. We all had our pictures, a short bio, and our sponsors listed in the local paper to introduce us to the world. But my answer to what I wanted to be in life, asked by the *Gong Show*-like emcee on stage, set me apart as well.

Good. My friend, the blonde beauty, walks on stage while I try to calm the very active butterflies in my stomach with an illegal piece of gum in my mouth and dodge the scrutiny of our hostess whose job it is make sure we are prepared to go on stage. Double pressure. What to do with the gum?

Most girls respond with definitive answers – actress, lawyer, doctor, and model, in no particular order. I don't aspire to any of those options. At seventeen and in the 1980s, did any girl, namely a small-town girl from West Virginia, really know what she wanted to do with her life? I did like writing for the school paper, so I figured I wanted to be a writer.

My friend answers. She wants to be "an actress (pause) with Tom Selleck in a red Ferrari."

The audience explodes with applause and laughter. She scored a home run, and I now have to follow.

I make the long walk through purgatory – stopping on my mark and hoping the wad of gum doesn't fall from the underside of my formal gown where I had stashed it. And then the million-dollar question is posed.

"Screenwriter." What?

The emcee looks puzzled. The audience is silent. It becomes what radio people refer to as the "dreaded dead air."

Desperate for the same applause that everyone else received, I add: "And write movies for Tom Selleck in a red Ferrari." Laughter, applause, laughter.

Whew. Just like a scene right out of an 80s film, I was relieved. Good thinking on my feet. Even the emcee recovered promptly.

The million-dollar question hung like a Mylar balloon later on the two-hour ride home from the pageant, but my family knows how to skirt an

10

issue that doesn't really pertain to us. Talk consisted of dresses, whose was prettiest, who they thought should've won, and the obligatory pat on the back of consolation for me for not winning. My mother and my grandmother didn't know how to become a screenwriter, and I surely didn't either.

Yes, I was the one who stayed until the lights came on at our one-screen movie theater, Groves Theater, beside our county courthouse, at one time the central hub of my hometown in West Virginia. Not just to watch the credits, with usually one of my cousins or sisters, but also to see the who's who of the balcony's older, popular crowd, descending the stairs with tousled hair. We also lingered to make Mom wait in the car and be part of the long parade down the one-way street, stretching out our much too short night out, before being dropped off at my Granny's where our short evening at Groves became a much longer night, stretching into the wee hours of the morning, watching *Chiller Theater* or amateur boxing on the small screen, and crunching chips in bed under the covers with a flashlight while telling ghost stories.

And yes, I was glued to Sunday night's *Wonderful World of Disney* with my three sisters, even though it aired on our fuzzy NBC channel and it often sent our dad out to 'the rock' behind the house, while the four of us would relay messages from the back-room window, through the kitchen, to the television to keep turning the antenna for a 'less snowy' picture at best. I recall lots of adventure stories with animals, but Disney had to compete with ABC (our only clear channel), and my Mom's choice of their Sunday Night Movie fare.

Since ABC's films ran until 11 pm, but my bedtime was set in stone at 10 o'clock, I would either beg to stay up or have to sneak into the kitchen doorway and listen to the intense dramas (make note filmmakers: sound is extremely important). Or, I would make several beelines to our only bathroom – with five women in the house, bear in mind – to catch a glimpse of the TV screen, prompting my Mom to assume I had a urinary tract or bowel problem. The television was within hearing distance of the porcelain throne, so I stretched out those Sunday night visits. (Again, filmmakers, sound is very important!)

This was the 70s, and the powerful epic of *The Ten Commandments* brought Sunday school stories to life like nobody's business, and, as I was from a family of Pentecostals preachers and church-goers (all great storytellers in their own right), scared the bejeesus out of me. And forget *Jaws,* one of my all-time favorites, however. It was *The Poseidon Adventure,* an intense, ocean-liner disaster film from 1972, starring Gene Hackman, Ernest Borgnine, Shelly Winters, and many others, where I realized the impact of film, and it still haunts me to this day. The Christmas tree topple, the final farewell by Winters – this film's powerful punch is probably why I've never been on a cruise ship to this day. Ah, the power of film when you couple the biblical epic with the disaster epic! Keep in mind that both of these films are adaptations.

That was just on television. I was obsessed with *Star Wars* (reading the tie-in book with pictures first), and then with a film that my sister's boyfriend took us to at his hometown theater – *Close Encounters of the Third Kind.* As a daughter born and raised deep in Appalachia, it was a thrill ride on screen to go to space, to the desert, and back – all in one sitting. (Yes, my sister eventually married that guy.) Did I somehow realize that someone wrote those films? Must have. I must have internalized it at some point.

I can't honestly say why I came up with "screenwriter" at the Strawberry Pageant, but I'm sure all of these childhood movie-going experiences influenced me, and luckily, every princess in the pageant received the same five-day, four-night stay at West Virginia Wesleyan

College, headquarters of the festival, along with access to all the festivities (to include a disco dance). That convinced me to get my college applications in, becoming the first in my family to graduate from college.

While at Marshall University on the West Virginia side of the Ohio River, I traded in my barely worn high heels from the pageant for Army boots, and I traded my princess status for cadet status in Army ROTC.

A natural career path for a screenwriter, right? Just join the Army. I wasn't the norm in pageants, and I wasn't going to be the norm for becoming a screenwriter either. However, I did become the first officer and the first woman in the Army in my family's long line of military service.

Even though I was an English major and I took a couple of creative writing courses, this was the 80s, and there were no film programs on most college campuses outside of LA and NYC, let alone a single screenwriting course. Not even close to what's out there today for wannabe film students and screenwriters. And I couldn't Google them if they had existed anyway – no Internet.

So, I became an active-duty tactical communications officer with a tour in Germany and helped bring down the Berlin Wall and, with it, Communism in 1989. With my remaining time in the reserves, I would go on to become a public affairs officer and write for *Soldiers* magazine, covering such stories as the Oklahoma City bombing aftermath and the Kosovo refugees' welcome to the U.S., and also go on to freelance for civilian publications.

Not a bad path as a writer, as I had the double duty of being an Army wife also and following my husband's career, ending up in such obscure places as Houghton, Michigan and Lawton, Oklahoma, where I could, however, at least take an occasional journalism class at a local college and write for newspapers and magazines, like *The Daily Oklahoman, Running Times,* and *New Jersey Bride.* We would also be assigned to Dayton, Ohio, where I was a stringer for the *Dayton Daily News* and attended the nearby Antioch Writers Workshop, where I also attended a joint screenwriting and playwriting seminar with a real live screenwriter on the panel – and a woman at that (not the norm I'd learn later on). Suzanne Clauser wrote for the TV show *Bonanza* and penned some films, to include an adaptation of her own novel, *A Girl Named Sooner.* She recommended if I couldn't live in L.A., to try another career path when I asked her for advice on how to be a screenwriter not living in L.A., or even anywhere near California. As an Army wife and a fairly new mom, I knew I would not be living there, so I had to find my own door to screenwriting. And like much advice I would be given through the years, I failed to heed it, knowing that most people outside of military life would never understand it. That, and, if someone tells me not to do something, I usually do the opposite.

I managed to write a couple of feature screenplays on my own using Syd Field's screenwriting books while living out on the Oklahoma prairie, directly across from the sixty-thousand acre Wichita Mountains Wildlife Refuge, where I'd also count buffalo in my spare time as well. My first script was a romantic drama to rival those ABC Sunday Night Movies (and will stay in my desk drawer forever), and then I penned a couple of romantic comedies, as I was heavily influenced by *Sleepless in Seattle* and other 90s romcoms.

After several Army moves and attempts at graduate school, I would finally enroll at the University of Oklahoma to pursue screenwriting and fiction under the Master of Liberal Studies program, after my own Army stint ended after twelve years. As an Army wife, you have to be creative -- I saw it as a chance to create my own screenwriting program. You make the most of what you have at the time, and I knew this was my shot at completing grad school and writing a creative thesis. In the MLS program, I studied fiction writing, feature-length screenwriting, film adaptation, and my selected area of gender in films -- military women portrayed in military films. My "tiny" thesis of 176 pages would gain a lot of mileage after grad school, and adaptation would play a significant role – in my writing life and in my Army life also.

If you would have asked me about this unplanned route to becoming a screenwriter, I wouldn't have had a clue that it would lead to any of the following stories, scripts, or a future film called *Angela's Decision*.

On to *Billy's Return*, my original short story. I was an avid reader growing up, too, and the Summersville Public Library, along with the movie theater, made my summers complete. (Oh, and the magnificent lake and Dairy Queens – we had two).

What inspired this story?

I was visiting my hometown one day from our first Army assignment, and I had gone to the movies with my sister. Yes, that same one screen in town (but soon to be replaced by a multiplex on the outskirts). I saw a guy we had gone to high school with coming out of the theater as I was in my car, turning onto that same one-way street. He wore his military uniform. His dress uniform, not BDUs. Air Force, I think. I was already a commissioned Second Lieutenant. I would never have thought to wear my own uniform at home, certainly not to the movies. In the Army then, we were strictly forbidden to wear our uniform to public places like that. (We were more isolated from the public due to carryover from Vietnam era). I was irritated. Maybe because as a woman, I doubted me in uniform would have the same effect as the one he prompted. At least in the way he did.

But I think it had the effect that he wanted. Attention. By girls and guys. So *Billy's Return* grew out of that incident and the "what if." What if a guy returns home from basic training, hometown hero-like, with "the girl" waiting for him? I knew that small town feeling also. Of waiting. Waiting for something big to happen. Waiting to leave, waiting to come back. I had also done plenty of waiting on my own husband by the time I would write this story over a decade later. Waiting for him to come home, waiting to hear that he was okay, waiting to move. That "what if" would became one of my graduate thesis components in the form of this short story.

LESSONS LEARNED: Nothing is ever for nothing in life, to include being a Strawberry Princess with gum stuck to her dress or numerous potty trips late at night to listen to TV movies your mom's watching while she folds laundry. If you can't go through the front door to your house of dreams, go through the back door, side door, crawl through a window, go down the chimney, or use the crawl space underneath and drill a hole through the floor. It's not always easy or fun, but breaking in will be worth it. And if you go to college and are lucky enough to study film and screenwriting from the get-go nowadays, don't forget to go out and make your own life stories. Those will come in handy one day, trust me.

2 BILLY'S RETURN

(The Short Story)

Billy lay spread eagle on his stomach on a Chicago Bears beach towel. His head ached from the party the night before. Too many Silver Bullets. The waves lapped against the lake's rocky shoreline set against the mountains in southern West Virginia. The rhythm lulled him between a nasty hangover and unconsciousness. Sleep, that's what he really needed.

His six-foot long body stretched off the towel, his feet sticking in some weeds. An open bag of Tostitos and empty Coke cans surrounded his head. The usually calm lake was violent because of a storm that had passed through in the wee hours of the morning, canceling part of his welcome home party. Billy didn't care. It was a warmer-than-usual November afternoon, and the sun filled his body with a warmth that he hadn't felt since leaving home in July. Not like the sticky heat of Fort Benning, Georgia. The kind that stays on top of your skin until you wash it off in a cold shower. This heat warmed him from the inside out.

In between bouts of consciousness, Billy had sworn the slicing waves were talking to him as they hit the bank, almost mocking him. *Krea...splash...Krea...splash...Krea...*

Billy felt a light tapping on his right leg. "Jacobs, get your ass out of the sack, now!"

He rolled over onto his back, startled out of half-sleep, a feeling he had become accustomed to during basic training. He shielded his eyes from the sun.

"Billy Jacobs, you wake up now. We ain't spent any time together since you got in yesterday," said a young woman.

His eyes finally focused. It wasn't his drill sergeant – it was only Angela. He should have been glad to see her. After all, he had been gone for weeks and that kind of training made you need somebody, anybody. But he should have waited until after the party to tell her that he wanted to wait another year to get married.

The cute, curly-headed blonde kicked some dead leaves on his legs. Her eyes were red and slightly puffy.

"Damnit, Angela, quit kickin' that crap on me. Good lord, do you know how many people probably pissed in those leaves last night? After all that beer?"

Billy sat up and brushed the leaves off his legs and towel. Angela took a bouncy step – she had been a cheerleader last year in high school – and sat next to Billy on the edge of his towel.

"Aren't you cold out here?" she asked, wiping leaves from her hands. Billy shook his head no.

He could tell Angela anything, and he knew she'd believe him. Even last night. After all of the crying, she finally accepted his decision that they should wait another year. At least for the moment. After all, he'd be gone for six months before they would even see each other again. And after the past twelve weeks, Billy knew that a lot could definitely change in six months.

"Last night was almost like old times. Almost. Something didn't seem, seem quite...," said Angela.

Billy held up his hand like a traffic cop. Angela fell silent and looked down. He felt sorry for her. He really did. She'd never know how he had outgrown Everly and the things in it. But one thing was for sure, he wasn't about to get sentimental over the past. He was on to a bright future.

He placed his finger under her chin, tilted her head, and kissed her lightly on the lips. Her cornflower blue eyes could still melt his heart, though. He placed her hand between his.

"Angie, I'm not the same. You wouldn't be either. The Army changes a man."

He spoke like the veteran of experience that he wasn't. Billy picked through the cans inside the small red cooler beside him until he found a Coke. He popped the top and took a drink. He knew Angie would think that he was at least trying to be sensitive. Angie took a deep breath.

"You know, Billy, that's all I've heard since you got back yesterday. Is it supposed to make me feel better to know that you've gotten out...?"

She stood up.

"I'd like to hear, 'I love you, Angie, I can't wait to get married, Angie.'"

She plopped down again and looked at Billy.

"You know, Billy. Life here <u>hasn't</u> changed for me. Still workin' at Murphy Mart, taken' one class at a time."

"I know, I know, Ange," said Billy softly. He took another drink and looked at the trees across the lake. The remaining leaves were dull, lifeless. It had been dry lately. Or, so he'd heard.

"Geez, do we have to go into this again?" Billy took her hand again. "I just want to save some money, Ange. All the guys I've talked to said they save a lot in Korea. You can get stuff real cheap."

Billy didn't need to say any more. She'd heard it all last night after he had drunk a few beers.

"You know, I could go with you, maybe."

"No, no, you can't. I have to live in the barracks."

"Not if we were married."

"God, Angela, I couldn't afford for both of us to live over there."

"I thought you said things were cheap?"

"Yeah, like clothes, Nikes and stuff. Not living there."

This wasn't like Angela. Billy couldn't understand why Angela was suddenly questioning his plans after three years together.

When they had graduated last year, she had wanted to get married, but he told her they should wait a year – work and save some money. He didn't want to go to the university like everyone else. He'd had enough football, and he didn't have the willpower to study.

Angela's cheerleading friends went off to college, and she stayed home and worked at Murphy Mart. Her real friends, though, ended up getting pregnant or getting married, staying in Everly. Angela had made the squad because of Billy. You never dated a Turner and didn't make the squad. His family didn't have a lot of money or anything, but the Turners had started this town, and his grandpa had helped build the manmade lake after he had come back from the War.

Billy's grandpa got him a construction job, but it didn't satisfy him. So, he ended up giving the community college a try, still living at home with his mother. Angela started classes, too. But Billy knew college wasn't for him, so he dropped out after two weeks. He told her to stay in, so she did. She'd do anything for him.

"Well, I guess you know best, Billy. If you want me to wait here, I will," she said, shrugging her shoulders.

Billy jumped up. He felt better after finishing his Coke. He grabbed her by the hands and pulled her up. He shook the leaves off the towel. She stood there with her hands on her hips.

"Let's go for a drive. My head feels better," said Billy.

Billy drove his red Suzuki Sidekick up the winding dirt road, away from their favorite spot at Turner Lake. It was usually everyone's favorite spot at one time or another. Angela was silent. Billy could always tell when she was pouting. Her lower lip stuck out just enough from her upper lip. That look had gotten her many things over the past three years, but marriage wasn't going to be one of them.

Billy reached for her hand after he shifted into second gear. He couldn't tell if the bump in the road knocked her hand away or if she jerked it away from his.

"Look, let's not ruin my two weeks home. We'll do anything you want. Promise," he said, trying to make up for the last twenty-four hours. He decided he really needed her right now. He kissed her hand. "Okay?"

"'Kay," she answered in her baby voice.

Billy dropped Angela off in front of variety store. He was glad that she couldn't get off work today. He needed time to be alone after being around soldiers the past three months. And as soon as the crowd heard he was home last night, they'd organized an impromptu party at the lake. It was mostly the seniors at school, since his crowd had either gone to one of the state colleges to play ball or had gotten married. But the seniors still looked up to him. He felt sorry for them – the Tigers hadn't won a game all season. If he had to give them a reason to party, then things were even worse around there than he thought.

Angela ran around to Billy's window. She was in a better mood since they'd made out in his new car. He bought it with his own money that he saved since he joined the Army. It was nice to be making payments on something, even though he'd have to leave the Sidekick at home while he was in Korea.

"Want me to pick you up after work?" he asked, leaning out the window.

"No, Jake will drop me off," said Angela.

She leaned in and gave him a kiss. He watched her walk across the parking lot. He thought nineteen looked good on Angela and was glad she'd kept her figure. He'd seen Nancy Edwards at the party last night and now he knew what the "freshman ten" meant. Only hers looked more like twenty.

Billy pulled in the driveway of the modest four-bedroom farmhouse. A man was standing on a ladder, painting the front a light blue. New black shutters were leaning against the front porch. He'd lived in this house from the time he was four until he started junior high. When his father died, his mother moved him and his brother, Jessie, in with her parents. Jessie was a junior this year. They later moved into town, so his mother could be closer to work. She was president of the local chamber of commerce.

The small farm was no longer a working dairy farm. Besides two of Grandpa Tucker's prize cows, an old dog and some cats, no animals resided on the property. The henhouse had been torn down when Grandma opened up a restaurant in town, and the barn only housed some junk. There wasn't any point in Grandpa keeping up a farm when nobody else showed an interest. The larger dairy nearby had kept up with the technology needed to mass produce. Now, Grandpa kept himself busy with what Grandma called "projects." He had retired from the Corps of Engineer a few years ago and had been restless since then.

The old man stopped painting when he heard Billy slam the car door. He cautiously backed down the ladder and laid the paint roller in the tin pan. Billy grabbed a paper bag off the dash and got out of the vehicle.

"Well, there's my boy," he said, as he walked towards Billy and shook his hand. He slapped Billy on the back. "Hah, I knew you'd make it through all that training. When'd ya' get in? How was the chow? Do they still have that black walnut ice cream like they used to? Boy, I sure do remember that black walnut ice cream. With real nuts, none of this imitation flavor stuff like Grandma buys."

They walked towards the wood shed in the back of the house. Grandpa wiped his forehead with a handkerchief. Billy smiled, embarrassed that his grandpa was so glad to see him, even though he was glad to see the old man himself.

"Oh, Grandpa, you know they stopped serving that ice cream after the last Great War." He liked to humor Grandpa.

"Oh, sure. Ain't been a war like that again. Don't you worry, though, those politicians will be out soon enough."

"How's things been around here? How's Grandma?"

"Oh, she's gettin' by. She's the favorite down at the physical therapy place. They all think she's making real progress from that there stroke."

They stop behind the woodshed. Grandpa took out his favorite lighter. It was a silver one. Billy took a box of cigars out of the bag and gave one to Grandpa. He held it up to his nose and took a long breath in, and then he bit off a piece and tasted it. He held it in his mouth for a minute, and then spat it out. Billy watched and waited.

"Yep, it's a good one. Let's light 'er up."

Billy took the silver lighter and lit Grandpa's cigar, then he lit one for himself. They lifted their cigars up in the air, as if they were toasting a glass of champagne.

Grandpa wasn't supposed to smoke anymore, but he decided that special occasions didn't count. And this was indeed a special occasion for Grandpa Turner, to have his grandson finish basic and be back home for at least a little while. Billy couldn't deprive him of a little smoke -- some things were still sacred between the men. They hid behind the woodshed, even though nobody else was home, out of fear that a passerby would spot them and tell Grandma. That's what happened in a small town like this, especially since Grandpa was still on the school board.

"Well, I'm glad you came by. So, you changed your mind about marryin' that Angie girl again?"

"Yeah, I told her last night that I wanted to wait 'til I got back from Korea. You know, save some money and all that."

Billy looked down and kicked at the dirt.

"Well, I can't say that I blame you for that. Younger folks got a lot more choices nowadays."

Grandpa started coughing as he blew the smoke out of his mouth. Billy knew that he'd probably had enough.

"Let's take a walk upon the ridge, Grandpa. I've missed the hickory and oak trees, the mountains. That damn Georgia just had some kind of tall pines. Pines and swamp."

Grandpa stamped out his cigar in the dirt, and then Billy dug a hole with a nearby shovel and buried their evidence.

"Yeah, I remember Georgia. Not much difference between that part of Georgia and Alabama. Still have the drop zone in Bama?"

Billy nodded. They slowly walked up an overgrown path to a level spot in the woods. Grandpa carried a walking stick. Billy looked at the tree line across the valley. The town was situated in the next valley over. Billy thought the woods smelled like chestnuts and cotton candy mixed together. He wondered what Angela was doing right now.

"You know, Bill, you better watch what you do here, while you're on leave," said Grandpa, almost reading Billy's thoughts. "That girl might have ideas, and then you would be in a fix."

Billy's face turned a light shade of red.

"Now I know what's on a young man's mind, things ain't changed that much. Still know that a uniform will drive a girl wild. And you come home feeling like you been through hell and survived it, start messin' with a girl's feelings."

24

Billy watched as a squirrel ran down a tree, hesitated, sniffed, and then ran back up and jumped to a neighboring oak. He knew not to interrupt Grandpa during one of his lectures.

Grandpa started coughing again. He reached in to his shirt pocket and took a drink of prescription cough medicine.

"You okay, Grandpa?"

"Oh, just a little hack I got. Now as I was sayin'. You're grown up enough to decide what you want. But you just watch that passion doesn't get too heated up for you not to use your brain," he said, lightly knocking Billy on the head with his fist.

"I sure don't want kids right now. I just, just want to see what's out there right now. And Angie, she don't understand that."

"Well, there's nothing wrong with stayin' right here and making a life, but I know how you feel, son. Just go and get it outta' your system. Korea'll be good for you," he said. "Sure, we'll miss you around here, but you do what you have to. Just don't string that girl along forever, 'cause I bet she won't wait too much longer."

He put his thumbs in the straps of his overalls and surveyed the land. They stood still and listened to a rustle in the bushes. Billy watched as Grandpa put his hands to his mouth and let out a turkey call. Billy never had mastered that trick.

"Well, at least you'll be here for squirrel season. Shorty and some of the boys are coming over next Saturday, and I expect you to be here."

"Yes, sir, I'll be here."

"Damn, Billy, what is your problem tonight? You haven't so much given me a kiss on the cheek. Don't it make you want me, knowing that you're gonna be across the world next week?" said Angela, irritated at being rejected by Billy for the second night in a row. "Look, I have to get to work

— I can enjoy the view here anytime."

Billy gripped the steering wheel of the Sidekick and gritted his teeth. The lake was calm this evening.

"What is that supposed to mean? Who have you been up here enjoying the view with while I been gone?"

"I'm going to ignore that remark, Bill Turner. Now take me to work," said Angela as she placed her blue smock on over her white rib-knitted shirt. She zipped up her blue jeans, catching the shirt. "Oh, damn!"

Billy placed his arm across the back of his seat and turned towards Angela. She struggled with the zipper. Billy had been afraid to make love with Angela, since Grandpa had planted the seed of doubt in his mind about her trying to get pregnant. He looked at himself in the rearview mirror and rubbed his head. His brown hair was starting to grow back in.

"I'm sorry, Angie. I'm just tired. You know Grandpa has me working my ass off since I got back home," he said, leaning over and kissing her on the cheek. "I'll pick you up after work and we'll go someplace else. How about the falls, okay?"

"Jake is taking me home after work."

"Well, fine. Tell Jake that he can screw you on the way home, too."

He brushed his hand on the top of his head, a habit he picked up in basic. Jake Gimble was a senior, and he lived beside Angela. Billy didn't really feel threatened by the skinny, pimply-faced guy. He just wanted to make Angela think that things were still the same for a little while longer, make her think he could still get jealous of other guys she knew.

Angela was silent. There went the lower lip again. He pulled her towards him, while she tried to pull away.

"I'm sorry. Look, tell him that I'm picking you up. Okay?"

"No, I have to get home tonight and help Susan with the baby."

Angela's cousin, Susan, lived with Angela and her parents, since her parents kicked her out for getting pregnant. She had the baby a month ago, and her parents still hadn't made an offer for her to come home. Billy hoped that Angela wasn't getting any ideas.

"Well, okay. What about tomorrow?"

"I have plans tomorrow with Susan. She really needs some help you know." She finally got her jeans zipped up.

"Okay, day after tomorrow, okay?"

She kissed him on the cheeks and rubbed his head. She had forgiven him.

"'Kay. I have a surprise for you anyway. You want to be with me more than anything, don't you, Bill?"

"Sure, Ange, you know I do," he said, hoping that she wasn't beginning to see his true feelings. Just one more week, and he'd be gone. Still, it would be nice to have Angie waiting for him when he went on leave again.

"Well, I think I know how we can do that."

A surge of panic ran through his body. Did she really want to get pregnant now? He tried to recall if he'd had a leak in his condom last Saturday night or not. No, no, it was Sunday, and Monday night they did it. He had made sure it was on correctly. God, he wondered if he could cut his leave short and go to Korea earlier. Angela must have seen the look of panic on his face.

"Relax, Billy. I've put the wedding magazines back in my drawer until next year. You were right, we should wait until you're finished in Korea."

He breathed a sigh of relief. He started up the car and shifted it in reverse.

Why couldn't he just break it off now, instead of waiting until next year? Billy was a nervous wreck waiting for Angela to get to his house. He had gotten his Class A uniform back from the cleaners yesterday and was brushing off a couple pieces of lint. He still had a week left at home, but not knowing what Angela had planned made him start preparing earlier. She better hurry up, he had a date to go hunting with Grandpa and the other men he had invited. And they hated for you to be late.

The door was open. He didn't want to wake his mother and brother with the doorbell when Angela arrived.

Click...click...click...click. Angela had on her boots with the high heels, walking up the sidewalk. Damn, tell her or wait, what's it going to be? He looked in the mirror on the hallway closet door. He thought he looked older. He had on a shirt Angela had bought for him last year. It felt too tight. What if she's pregnant? Nah, couldn't tell so soon. Or could you?

"Billy? Billy, come on out. I don't want to wake anyone up," whispered Angela through the screen door.

Billy took a deep breath and turned around. He pushed the door open, catching it before it slammed. Angela was sitting on the steps. He sat down beside her and rubbed his hands nervously. He saw his breath in the cool morning air. Great hunting weather.

"What's up that couldn't wait until this afternoon?" said Billy rather coolly.

She took a deep breath. It didn't look good for him.

"Well, I've been thinking a lot since you got back."

Was she going to put the blame on him now for screwing up her life? She turned to look at Billy. Her eyes were all red, like she'd been watching *Old Yeller* and crying for a long time.

"I've watched how hard it's been for Susan. And I've seen a change in you, Bill, something that I've been trying to understand. Maybe you've decided you don't want me after all..."

"Now, Ange...."

"Let me finish."

He looked at her, then looked away. He made rings with his breath. He looked at his watch. Zero six-thirty hours, Army time. Grandpa was probably having a fit. He wondered if you could hunt in Korea. Did they even have squirrels?

"Things aren't just the same anymore, Bill. I thought you were gonna be my way out this place, but you're right. I need to take charge of my own life," she stopped suddenly. "Oh, look at that cute little chipmunk, Billy."

Billy watched as the animal scurried up the maple tree in front of the house, scrounging for winter. He'd been saying these things to her in a roundabout way for the past year. This seemed to be a funny way of telling a guy that you're pregnant, he thought.

"Angie... would you just tell me..."

She took a piece of paper out of her jacket pocket and thrust it into his hands.

"Here, just take a look. Make sure I didn't sign up for anything crazy."

Confused, he looked at the papers. Oh, he knew exactly what these papers meant. He was too stunned to say anything.

"I know, I know. You probably think it's crazy, or I'm crazy. At first, I thought maybe we could even be together, but I know you don't really want that, Bill."

"Ange..."

"Don't tell me I'm stupid. My mother already did. She's real pissed about it," said Angela, shrugging her shoulders.

The paperboy rode by on his bicycle and threw a newspaper. It landed at Billy's feet.

"I don't know what to say, Angela. You... you know this doesn't mean you'll get sent to Korea. I'll be on the DMZ, you'd be south of there, if you even got there at all," said Billy.

She grabbed the papers and jumped up. "I don't need a geography lesson, Billy."

"I didn't mean – "

"I'll even get to go in as an E-2 private because of my college credits."

Billy stood up, and they hugged for what seemed to be eternity. He held on to Angela like he never had before. Thoughts raced through his mind. She wouldn't be here when he got back in six months. His eyes teared up. She took the papers from his hand.

"We've just been foolin' each other, Billy. I don't want to end up like Susan or the other girls around here. I needed to get out, too," she said, as she twisted her salvation in her hands. "I have to go. You better go meet your Grandpa. I'll call you this evening. Okay?"

"'Kay," he responded hoarsely.

Billy sat back down on the steps and watched her walk away. The wind scattered some leaves on the sidewalk. He pulled up the collar on his shirt and blew on his hands to warm them. He wondered if it was cold in Korea this time of year, and if Grandpa had kept an extra cigar.

3 ON WRITING THE SCREENPLAY: ANGELA'S DECISION

I thought the best place to begin was with the short story, because it most approximates the dimensions of the average film. Novels tend to have too much material, but short stories contain all the basic elements a film needs in one package: character, plot, setting. Like movies, stories are to be consumed in one sitting. The good ones transport you, the great ones change you, and the bad ones – well, at least they are short.

-Francis Ford Coppola

It's pre-dawn in the wee hours of the morning at a tactical and training Army post in southwest Oklahoma, and we're approaching the gate at Fort Sill. We've just chaperoned our daughter's first Valentine's Day junior high dance where her dad had cut in on her and her first boyfriend to dance with his once-little girl to Christina Aguilera's "You Are Beautiful." That song would make me cry from now on. I feel like I'm trapped in a bad plotline in a film. But I'm not. The dance went well, but her dad's about to deploy in that first wave before the war even begins in Iraq in 2003.

At home after the dance, we just lay on the bed after he's done one last check of gear and stowed his duffle bags in the car. Our daughter goes back and forth to our room, finally settling down in her own room. We ignore the phone calls from home, as these are our last moments together for an indefinite period. Nobody feels like talking, not even to each other. He'll have a chance to call them back in a couple of days.

The elephant in the room sits heavy on my chest, as I turn to him and say: "In case, you don't come back, I need –"

"Shhh, I'm coming back."

"But –"

"But nothing, I'm coming back."

This hug is different, more like a blanket covering my entire soul. There is no crazy pre-deployment sex (as we would see portrayed in the stereotypical TV series *Over There* a year later). However, a thought of getting pregnant one last time enters my head full of other crazy, noisy ideas, but I push it away. I'm in graduate school now, and three is the magic number for us. Him, me, and her. I'm happy with that. Very happy. Until now, when it feels circumstances are ripping us apart, and I can't control any of it. Getting pregnant would be a form of control. Something an Army wife will rarely ever have, in her active-duty married life anyway.

We are at the gate. The gate guards search my mini-van – even higher ranking officers are subject to a vehicle search coming on post nowadays. Before 9-11, there weren't even guards on this gate, and we'd have just breezed right in, as would anyone else. After the Fall of the Wall and then in the 90s, we became a much more accessible Army, hoping to strengthen community bonds by opening our gates. Come one, come all, we have no secrets. But so much has changed since then for the country and most noticeably to those of us in the Army. And our life was about to change even more, just like our gates had.

Rail cars have been chugging out slowly all week, with Army vehicles and equipment strapped down. Everything has slowed in motion, to include camouflaged hearts. I have to remind myself to breathe. Going away ceremonies and tearful goodbyes dominant the news, with mostly women and children grasping the airport fence for one last look back at the boarding planes. This is interspersed with the political commentary of the day and the irrational scenes of people smashing Dixie Chicks CDs in the streets, some even by children, along with the burning of American flags in foreign countries. No room for in between. A one-size-fits all, for us or against us. Like ordering coffee, with cream or without, at the local diner.

What had brought politicians and the country together after 9-11 was tearing them apart for the build-up to Iraq. Talk of Freedom Fries and patriotism were woven together like a quilt, and the soldiers who were about to deploy would carry that along with their other baggage. The media, politicians, and the public assumed we were all of a singular opinion. Right or wrong, my Army generation, now mid-level leaders and higher, had grown up with the Powell Doctrine, and this was nowhere close. Those of us in the Army community would debate this in a different way than the newsmakers, causing a collective shudder when the then-Chairman of the Joint Chiefs of Staff, General Shinseki, and his advice would not be heeded on troop strength. That alone made me more nervous as a wife, because I, too, had trained under that doctrine during my time as a soldier.

His sense of urgency to just go and get the job done is coupled with my sense of helplessness and fear, making for a toxic combination ready to explode at the gate. I don't blame him for being irritated, but I'm glad for the lengthened stay of just ten minutes longer. Every moment counts now. His ceremony and parade will consist of a wife and daughter hugging him goodbye and then walking to the vehicle to join the others. Several times.

He's agitated at being searched. While he has no plane to catch, he is to meet a group of men, mostly civilians, who will convoy to another Army post in Georgia for a week's training and then fly to the big sandbox "over there," way ahead of the many young men and women from all parts of the country who would join him soon. He's the guy in charge – he can't be late. And it's time to stick the family into that compartment he uses – they're all taught to do that – in order to make his job easier. One mustn't think of home when that far away when one's on the brink of war.

With duffle bags in hand, he walks to join the others. I know I have to leave, but my foot is shaky on the gas pedal. I can't seem to press it down. Is the car in forward or reverse? No matter, the big parking lot just contains a few dark vehicles waiting to head out. I can go either way, forward or reverse, but I cannot go with him. Even though I am fully trained for war, I am no longer in the Army (thank God, as it would mean even more major upheaval for our daughter).

But still. Part of me longs to go. Not because I was ever eager to go to war. But if to just keep the pact we made as lieutenants that we would find each other on the battlefield if the shit ever hits the fan. I think back on those two kids who joined the Army and our reasons for doing so. The shit's about to hit the fan, I can't stop it, and I have to stay behind and keep the remaining pieces of our lives together at home.

The fact that he's not fenced off at the airport like most deployments with the obligatory fanfare makes me want to jump out of the car again and grab one last hug. But I've already done that twice -- I'm just making it harder – for the three of us.

"Mom, let's go." My daughter gently touches my arm, the not-so-tiny voice of nearly thirteen-year-old reason right now, giving me strength to finally push the gas. It's been just the two of us before many times, but now I need her commands to just force me away and to even take a breath.

We pass the gate where we were searched. The sun births a spectacular palate of blues, pinks, and oranges as we travel back home in silence. Daughter and mother, with hearts tethered together by war and by blood, weighed down like an anchor right now.

Back at home, I can't sleep, even without any sleep for two days now. I'll get used to this non-sleep mode during the war's early days. I'm also nauseous and hungry at the same time, but I cannot eat. I cannot sit still. Maybe there is still a chance that it won't really happen. It was like a bad dream sequence in a TV show, like the one in *Dallas*.

I take a deep breath. As I'll do many days to come. Because of her. There is a film screening at the University of Oklahoma in Norman later in the day. It's a 90-minute drive. I could just blow it off, not go. It's not mandatory, and my professor would understand. I grab my car keys and purse and rush into Ursula's room.

"Wanna go to Norman and see a film?"

"Sure." My young tower of strength seems solid and ready to crumble at the same time. But she's as much like him as me, and while I'm all over the global map of emotions, she contains her sadness, for now, and puts it in a compartment just like he does. Going to see my first animated film that was not made by Disney quiets my nerves. While he's driving off to war, we drive to the opposite of war.

I don't remember the drive at all. I just remember being soothed and moved at the same time by some animated film that I can't even remember the name of. I see war, I see sadness in it, and I see my emotions played out upon the screen. Of course. This is what film has always been to me, since I was a little girl. Not just an escape or entertainment, but a reflection or a prism of myself. Bits and pieces of me, on the big and small screen. A world can be torn apart and put back together in one sitting. On screen.

My thesis chair has a party at his home after the screening for the NYC-based filmmakers. They want to hear my take on the impending war. I get to speak openly. (Something I only do in closed circles in my Army town, as well as still order French fries no matter the crossed out menu item on the burger-as-large-as-your-plate landmark I go to.) I debate for going to war and why we shouldn't – both at the same time. I will go to

35

many of these "Writers' Block" parties (as my thesis chair dubs them) while he's deployed. That, coupled with writing and going to the local mall movie-plex, are my own compartments for war, and my film one expands during deployment – from Will Ferrell's comedy *Old School* as the lone female with a theater full of male Army trainees to rocking with Jack Black in *School of Rock* to more sobering indie fare, such as Sophia Coppola and Scarlet Johansson's breakout film *Lost In Translation* and Evan Rachel Wood in Catherine Hardwicke's drama *Thirteen*. My daughter and I will see at least one film every week for the next year, even more during the first weeks of the war in Iraq. It seems I can only stand to sit still in a movie theater. It's the only place where I can breathe easier.

The nation pays attention when the regular network television programming is interrupted, and as one local coffee barista puts it so eloquently: "They've even stopped my soap operas this week for the war."

For Iraq. As Afghanistan is slowly banished from lead stories and moved to the crawlers on screen and to back page stories, making it seem, at least to the public, that our work is done "there" in that "over there."

The following weeks, I'll also drive on post many times and just put my thesis work aside, especially the romantic comedy script that I'm writing. I will drive by a remote parking lot full of vehicles, fenced off and chained with locks, everyday. These cars belong to soldiers who are deployed. Mainly young, single soldiers. They have no loved ones nearby to look after what is probably their most prized possession at the moment. And I wonder what their stories are. The owners of these cars and trucks.

I also see Billy and Angela reflected in the cars and in the faces at the Post Exchange (the Army's version of Wal-Mart but with some designer labels). I'll think about why they joined the army, just like we did. The vehicles come in all different sizes, shapes, and brands. Just like soldiers do.

No two are alike, even though we do train and deploy for the common mission at hand. We all have our own reasons for joining and even our own opinions on the war.

The political commentary will continue – soldiers will be used for photo ops and positions on war. But I know, as do Angela and Billy in *Billy's Return*, that the decision to join the Army is as varied as we are, and while patriotism may frame the decision to join, it is not usually the single draw to the military, as politicians and media would have one believe. That would provide a frame for my remaining thesis work, as well as the "what if."

While I write this book about adaptation, it is not my intent to critique my own work or become a full-fledged how-to or textbook. This is about my journey. I did study adaptation in grad school, using James Naremore's book, *Film Adaptation*, which contains valuable essays and theories about adaptation. However, next, I offer the reader the opportunity to read the short story, *Billy's Return*, and then read the screenplay, *Angela's Decision*, allowing the reader to see the metamorphosis, pick it apart, and subsequently compare the two. Then, ultimately, watch the film, *Angela's Decision*, and compare the three. It's rare that the viewer gets to read the original, adapted screenplay, as the shooting scripts are the ones readily available, and then the final film becomes its own entity. Again, it's up to the reader to decide in which order to read or view. But starting with story to script to film allows the reader to understand the original progression of the adaptation. The reader may also choose to skip the introductions to each and then go back to read those once the adaptation "process" is complete.

I had written *Billy's Return* from the male point-of-view of a young man joining the army, and his return to his hometown after basic training. At the time I'd written that story, we were already entrenched in Afghanistan and making progress. An old parachuting injury in the Army caused chronic pain that had cut my career short, and I was two years into a graduate program for screenwriting and fiction at OU in 2003.

I was fifty pages into writing a feature length screenplay of about a hundred pages – a holiday romantic comedy meant to complete my thesis. With my husband set to deploy in a couple of weeks, I couldn't concentrate, and I certainly couldn't find the funny in anything. With my thesis deadline looming and only a minimum requirement of a sixty-page thesis needed, which I already had with two short stories and half of a feature script that I would later finish, I decided to alter the path of my thesis.

My thesis was due in just a couple of months. However, the short story, *Billy's Return*, really bothered me. I really didn't like it, and something about it just kept nagging at me.

Professor J. Madison Davis, who'd been my independent study professor for the short story, suggested that I write it as a short script from Angela's point-of-view because of the nature of the ending. He also knew I had taken another independent study class with Professor Joanne Rapf, which allowed me to study adaptation and a gender-in-film study of military women portrayed in military films from WWII to the 1990s. Combine those with my feature writing independent study and it all came together. Of course! Why hadn't I thought of that sooner? Another script.

My thesis chair and screenwriting professor, Andy Horton, allowed me to add one more project to my already double-sized thesis. As I stated earlier, nothing is ever for nothing – I adapted *Billy's Return* into *Angela's Decision*, a short script of 40 pages. My short story set in the mid-80s in small town West Virginia became a short script set in the mid-80s in small town Oklahoma

While menus were being changed from French fries to Freedom fries and other displays of patriotism from the comforts of home, I felt that nobody really understood <u>what</u> drew young men and women to join the military, especially the Army, and why they'd put their lives on the line, nor did they want to know. They deemed us all patriots, and we were to just do our duty, which we do, no matter our own thoughts on the war. I did not want to debate that in a story, but I did want to show who these young men and women are and the <u>why</u> of joining the army, without the trappings of patriotism. Other films already try to capture that. I wanted to show the decision to join.

And as always (anytime the media spotlight shines on soldiers) there was also talk, again, of how women, especially mothers, should not be in the military. We couldn't handle it. As a matter of fact, after I wrote my adaptation, newspaper columnist Phyllis Schlafly would write a scathing column condemning mothers who were soldiers and in Iraq (barely two months into the war and near Mother's Day). I had been a soldier and a mother for a short time while in the Army, and the desire to serve my country was no less strong than my husband's. They weren't questioning fathers. This made me angry. My study of military women portrayed in military films came in handy. We had come a long way, but this column was just a bad attempt to play at America's heartstrings and declare women shouldn't be in the military, namely the Army or Marines on the ground, at all.

That debate about women in the Army continued, even though women in one unit proved they could fight and die for their country. Army specialist Lori Piestewa would die trying to save her unit after they took a wrong turn in Iraq, as she was trying to fend off a ruthless enemy. In the same unit, her best friend, Jessica Lynch, would be taken as a POW and later rescued. All adding more fuel to the debate of sending women into combat, even though many women proved over and over again that they could handle the rigors of war on par with men. What many failed to understand was that women were an integral part of going to war, and the missions could not be done without them anymore. About fifteen percent of the Army was now women, and <u>all</u> jobs became combat jobs in war zones, especially this one.

Richard Krevolin, whom I'd meet at a writer's conference during this time, states in his book *Screenwriting For The Soul* that stories come to you when you are ready to receive them, and I was ready to receive *Angela's Decision*, as a screenplay. I was on my own mission, and if my husband could go to war, I could finish my thesis before he returned.

They say write what you know or what you want to read, or see, in this case. So I did. I wrote *Angela's Decision* in three days, just two weeks before my own husband deployed, before the war even began.

I wrote *Billy's Return* from Billy's point-of-view about a small town, nineteen-year-old boy who returns to his hometown and girlfriend after completing his basic training, and before going to his first duty station in Korea. Angela Jacobs, his girlfriend, has waited on him with the hopes that he will marry her before he leaves. In that short story, I wanted to show how Billy had thought he had changed and the town and others had not, including Angela. *Billy's Return* is more about his internal struggle to keep Angela waiting for him in Everly than about Angela's actual decision, which is the surprise ending. I tried to show that Angela, only a supporting (but important) character, had invested so much time in waiting for Billy that she was the one that would make the greatest leap for change.

Having *Billy's Return* as a blueprint enabled me to write a first draft of *Angela's Decision* in a few days. I switched to Angela's point-of-view in the screenplay, and the words flowed just like tears, like the many I would shed.

An adaptation is not a play-by-play of the source material, like my short story. In Naremore's book, he discusses four theories of adaptation. I'll let the reader and viewer banter about which my script is after reading the original short story and Naremore's book. Naremore also provides a major statistic – over half of all films are adaptations. Even Francis Ford Coppola started his own short story magazine, *Zoetrope*. Many filmmakers and writers tout the advantages of adapting from a short story. Horton states in his own books about screenwriting that beginning screenwriters would be best off starting with a short story or novel.

Horton, who approved my adaptation of *Billy's Return* to include in my thesis, said an adaptation can surpass the original material. I think that is certainly true of my adaptation of *Billy's Return*, but the reader and viewer must be the judge. No short story adaptation to script can be a word-for-word account of the original, what film critics often refer to as fidelity to the original work.

In *Angela's Decision*, we see more of Angela's life and how she came to the decision she made. Decisions. Plural. The town is introduced as a character of despair. Minor characters are introduced, and some are expanded to help propel Angela towards her decision. Susan, a character just mentioned in conversation in *Billy's Return*, for example, becomes a catalyst and a mirror of sorts for Angela's life.

There is an old saying about why people join the Army -- you're either running from something or running to something. In the script *Angela's Decision*, we see both. Angela makes a life-changing decision in both stories, but in *Angela's Decision*, we actually see what she is giving up and possibly gaining by her decision, with the same surprise ending in both the script and the short story. And we see them all make decisions, not just Angela.

I heeded my thesis chair's advice of the carnivalesque in writing the

41

script – that process towards becoming in its purest form. It is the time when no rules hold, or, rather, when one can become whatever he or she wishes, allowing the character and story to become, instead of imposing structure. Sherman Alexie's *Smoke Signals: A Screenplay* would become a study guide for me – I would even meet director Chris Eyre at an OU film event as I completed my thesis in Spring of 2003.

I also added a twist to *Angela's Decision* for the thesis version. I added an alternative ending with Angela in her new setting – Army basic training. Since the script was 40 pages, I nearly had a television drama length script, and with the addition of the ending of her new location, I felt it could be promoted as a TV pilot. All those Sunday night trips to the bathroom, listening to TV dramas, as a girl might pay off finally.

My idea for a television series started to take shape. I wanted to show young people, like Angela and Billy, not only making the decision to enter the military, but also follow Angela and Billy and others in the military, showing how high-level decisions filter down to their level, along with the decisions they'd have to make each and every day while in the Army. I thought of all of those vehicles in the parking lot at Fort Sill again. When you go to war, and even in garrison, every decision, large or small, counts and can affect the person next to you in the foxhole, or, as in the case of Iraq, in the sandbox. I would also have discussions during this time with new lieutenants training at Fort Sill and talking of their decisions to join the army, how the war would transition to a war of insurgency and IEDs (as my own husband would still be there to witness), and how ill-prepared they felt they were to even go to war at all. These were topics at local cafes and they confided in me as a veteran and as the wife of a leader already "over there." This gave me more of a sense of urgency to complete my thesis.

Before being bound in my thesis, *Angela's Decision* became an award-winning script. It had also been read by a cable network executive after I pitched it as a TV series pilot at the then-annual Screenwriting Conference in Santa Fe (now defunct). My daughter and I had road-tripped to Santa Fe while her dad was still deployed. While other writers there prepped and worried about the two or three producers they would pitch to, I prepared my pitches for the entire block of over a dozen producers. I knew I would never have this chance to be side-by-side with Hollywood producers again (though that has changed now with pitch sessions in LA). May and June 2003 would become busy months for us both, as that was best during deployment, to just stay busy because once again, I was waiting. Waiting for war to end, waiting for him to be okay and come home, and waiting to make yet another Army move. And I'd be damned if I left without my diploma and thesis in hand, after making other moves in mid-studies.

Ursula and I would also go to another writer's conference in Oklahoma City, where another script of mine, a romantic comedy, would place second in a writer's contest, and I would meet writer Richard Krevolin, by volunteering to assist him while there. During that writer's conference and on my daughter's birthday, it's announced on the news that the war may be ending, as President George W. Bush stands before the unfurled banner of "Mission Accomplished" on a Navy ship. I can't concentrate, so what do we do that night? We go see a movie with Krevolin and writer Colleen Sell (my daughter's first R-rated film, and, later, in Santa Fe, she'll get purple streaked-hair to match her own war time moods).

A few days later, my husband would call and say: "Don't believe what you're hearing on the news." As *Billy's Return* would change and be adapted into the script *Angela's Decision*, the war was not over, and our enemies would adapt, with Iraq evolving into a different type of war.

I wasn't sure what he meant at the time, but months and years later, I would certainly know that what he said was true, as would our Billy's and Angela's in the military and the rest of the world.

LESSONS LEARNED: See chapter one and repeat those lessons learned. Instead, I have listed the books that influenced me in graduate school and specifically while writing my thesis:

Sherman Alexie's *Smoke Signals: A Screenplay* (My screenplay spirit guide. I'd meet the film's director Chris Eyre at a film event at OU in 2003).

Madeline DiMaggio - *How to Write for Television*

Lajos Egri - *The Art of Dramatic Writing*

Andrew Horton - *Laughing Out Loud: Writing the Comedy and Writing the Character Centered Screenplay*. His guidance, along with my other professors, would prove invaluable.

Lew Hunter - *Screenwriting 434* (I would meet him at an OU event)

Richard Krevolin - *Screenwriting from the Soul*

James Naremore - *Film Adaptation*

Dwight Swain -*The Techniques of the Selling Writer* (another one of OU's own)

Kristin Thompson - *Storytelling in the New Hollywood* (about the four act structure, typical of TV dramas, except ABC dramas now use six acts)

Barbara Ueland - *If You Want to Write: A Book About Art, Independence and Spirit*

4 ANGELA'S DECISION
(The Screenplay)

FADE IN:

EXT. ANGELA'S HOUSE - 1987 – MORNING

A small, rundown one-story house sits on the edge of Everly, a small dying town in Oklahoma. The front yard alternates between patches of weeds and junk. The other houses on the street look the same on this ugly November day.

INT. ANGELA'S BEDROOM – DAY

An old, beat-up dresser looks like a beautician's work station gone wild -- make-up, different size hairbrushes, curlers, and a curling iron. In the clutter stands a cheerleading trophy, a track runner's trophy, and some PICTURES of teenage friends.

POSTERS of places, like Germany, Switzerland, and Hawaii, adorn the walls of bedroom. A framed college acceptance LETTER hangs tilted. Blankets are thrown across a twin-size bed.

ANGELA JACOBS, 18, wears the small town dress code well -- tight jeans, tight red sweater, and heels. She stands looking into the mirror, trying to pull her long, semi-permed, bleached blonde hair into a ponytail.

Angela has a beauty beneath her too-old-for-her-age fatigue. She sighs at her reflection. A HORN HONKS outside.

ANGELA: Shit. Just a minute.

ANGELA grabs her BLUE WORK SMOCK (Wal-Mart-like) and puts it on. She grabs some make-up, brush, and hair spray, and stuffs them into her purse.

She knocks over a PHOTO of herself, in cheerleader's outfit, and her boyfriend, BILLY TURNER, then 16, in football uniform. She places it beside a recent PHOTO of Billy in his Army uniform. Angela hurries.

INT. LIVING ROOM - DAY

LINDA JACOBS, *Angela's mother, 37, sleeps in a chair, grasping a cigarette in one hand and a bottle of Vodka in the other. Still dressed from what appears to be a night on the town at the local honky-tonk, Linda doesn't move as the RADIO PLAYS an old country tune.*

Angela stands and stares at Linda, disappointed. We sense this is routine for Angela. She removes the cigarette, grinds it into a nearby ashtray. She turns OFF the radio. Angela takes pity and covers Linda with a shabby blanket.

Linda wakes up and grabs Angela's hand.

LINDA: Where the hell you goin'?

Angela pulls away.

ANGELA: I'm going to work.

Angela throws the blanket.

ANGELA: (*to herself*) Which is more than I can say about you.

Linda tries to get up, but falls back into the chair.

LINDA: I worked all night. At the pool hall.

ANGELA: Yeah, work.

LINDA: Better than stackin' tampons all day.

Linda rubs her head.

LINDA: Where's Jenny?

Linda pulls some money out of her bra. Angela, disgusted, turns to leave.

ANGELA: You dropped her off at Grandma's... last week.

LINDA: So, Mr. Big Shot comes back to town today. And now you're Miss High and Mighty. You better watch yourself.

Linda pulls herself out of the chair. Angela rushes out the door.

LINDA: Hey, you hear me?

46

EXT. ANGELA'S HOUSE - DAY

Linda follows Angela to the doorway. A car idles by the curb.

LINDA: I don't need no babies around here. He ain't gonna' marry the likes of you, girl.

Linda tries to straighten up, waves to the car.

LINDA: Hey Susan, nice to see ya'.

Angela rushes to Susan's car.

INT. SUSAN'S CAR – DAY

Angela slams the passenger door shut. SUSAN RANDALL, *18, dressed in the same* BLUE SMOCK *underneath her coat, waves to Linda, then reaches back to check on one-year-old* TOM JUNIOR *in his car seat.*

SUSAN: It's okay, sweetie.

Susan places a pacifier in Junior's mouth. She checks herself in the rearview mirror, runs her hand through her short, brown hair.

SUSAN: He's teething again. I see your Mom is friendly as ever.

Angela sits, fuming.

ANGELA: Yeah, I guess she's the friendliest gal in town.

Angela watches Linda on the porch, holding onto the rail. Looks back at Susan.

ANGELA: Nice cut. Janice do it?

Susan nods and smiles, pulling car out onto the road.

 SUSAN: She is right about one thing. We don't need any more babies around here.

They look at each other, burst out LAUGHING.

INT. VARIETY STORE – DAY

Angela stocks packages of toilet paper on a shelf. They fall down on top of and around her. Her up-tight supervisor, MR. VINSON, *40s, peers around the corner with a clipboard, shaking his head. He moves on down the aisle.*

47

Angela sticks out her tongue and makes a face at him. She looks at the toilet paper on the floor, checks her watch.

INT. LADIES' CLOTHING DEPARTMENT – DAY

Angela arranges a rack of clothes in the ladies' department. She picks up a PILLOW misplaced on top of one of the racks. She starts to take it back to the houseware department, then notices a full-length mirror.

Angela stands in front of the mirror, places the pillow under her smock, and poses.

Susan turns the corner and drops an armful of clothes as she sees Angela. Angela, smiling, looks at Susan.

ANGELA: How does this look on me, Ma'am?

Susan grabs the pillow and hits Angela with it.

SUSAN: Better fit up here, Ma'am.

Susan places it under her smock and pushes it up to her chest. Mr. Vinson sneaks up on them.

MR. VINSON: Miss Jacobs and Mrs. Randall, get back to work. Someone around here'll want a paycheck.

He marks something on his clipboard and EXITS. Angela mimics him. Susan laughs, picks up clothes. A moment of SILENCE, as Angela caresses the pillow.

SUSAN: You promised you wouldn't do anything stupid, right?

ANGELA: I know. I know.

Susan leaves with the armload of clothes. Angela looks into the mirror, placing the pillow under her smock one more time.

INT. PIZZA PARLOR - NIGHT

Booths line two of the walls in this hole-in-the-wall pizza and beer joint. Angela stands BY THE JUKEBOX, drinking a beer, trying to make a selection.

In center of the room, tables are pushed together to accommodate a large group of GUYS, various ages, surrounding BILLY TURNER, 19, sporting his dress green Army uniform, Class A's. Empty pizza pans and pitchers of beer litter the table. Their LAUGHTER echoes through the room. They are THE crowd tonight.

The handsome and physically fit Billy takes off his Army jacket and flings it over the only empty chair. He looks like an Army poster of the new recruit that he is, just home from basic.

TOM RANDALL, *Susan's husband, and* KEVIN SCOTT, *both 19 and Billy's best friends, sit drinking beer. They're enthralled with Billy's stories, as all are. The only oddity at the table is Susan and Tom Junior, sitting outside the circle of guys, behind Tom.*

The middle-aged COOK, *male, the two waitresses,* JENNY, *30, and* IMOGENE, *50, and the high school busboy,* HANK, *look like part of the permanent fixtures, once new, but now neglected. Hank still retains his youth, but is tired-looking. He is bussing the table, trying to get a good look at Billy.*

Angela keeps looking at Billy. Billy nods at Angela from across the room. She acknowledges him by raising her beer.

Junior gets fussy. Susan pokes at Tom, but he ignores her. Angela watches Susan get up, with the Junior on her hip, and walk to the jukebox. MUSIC PLAYS.

SUSAN: They can't go on much longer, can they?

ANGELA: What are they talking about now? Let me guess. Football?

SUSAN: I need to get Junior home. If anyone can break it up, you can.

Susan bounces Junior.

SUSAN: Surely, Billy is horny after bein' around nothin' but guys for weeks. And you? Well, you just better...

Junior gets louder.

ANGELA: Here, let me have him.

Angela takes Junior and bounces him, kisses him. She catches Billy watching her.

Imogene walks up behind Angela. Imogene plays with the baby.

IMOGENE: Better watch it, those are contagious 'round here. Sure is a handsome sight.

SUSAN: Thanks.

Imogene points over to Billy.

IMOGENE: I was talkin' about hers, over there. Though this one's already a lady killer.

Susan gives Imogene a friendly shove.

IMOGENE: You ladies like a refill? On them?

AT BILLY'S TABLE, Billy looks over at Angela, takes a drink of beer, laughs at one of the guys. Hank busses the table, trying to catch some remnants of the conversation.

TOM: You should have seen Troy at the alumni game this year.

Hank knocks over a near-empty glass, landing near Billy. Tom gives Hank an evil look.

TOM: Hey, stupid. You know who you almost spilled that shit on?

The table QUIETS down. Hank looks like he's going to crap his pants.

HANK: Don't everybody know who Billy Turner is?

Tom stares the kid down. Billy beams at the recognition.

TOM: You need to take notes, kid. Pull up a chair.

Hank looks back at Cook, hesitates.

HANK: But...

TOM: I said sit down.

The Cook nods yes to Hank, to sit down.

BILLY: Tom, it's okay. What's your name?

HANK: Hank.

TOM: Now where was I? The Class of '82 ate dirt. Go ahead, Billy.

AT THE JUKEBOX, Angela hands junior back to Susan. Susan takes him, walks to the table and sits in the chair with Billy's jacket.

AT BILLY'S TABLE, Angela follows Susan and stands behind Billy.

BILLY: Well, they needed someone for their scrimmage game, right? Against the officers, West Pointers.

KEVIN: Oh, no. Here it comes.

BILLY: And the Drill Sergeant comes up to me and says, "Turner ever carry a football?"

The guys LAUGH. Hank, on the edge of his seat, looks like he's witnessing the second coming of Christ.

Angela tries to pull Billy away. He pushes her hand away. She pulls up a chair and sits beside Susan. Angela and Susan look at each other, bored.

TOM: Ever carry a football? That's a good one.

BILLY: Yeah, I know. And I said, yes, Drill Sergeant. Carried one all the way to state champs two years ago.

The guys LAUGH again.

KEVIN: Man, you should be at the university, Billy.

The laughing subsides.

BILLY: Yeah, well the Army's gonna pay for college.

TOM: And the university can stick it up their ass. Imagine takin' away a scholarship because of one grade. I'd have caught that professor and...

Tom smacks a fist into the palm of his other hand. Billy looks at the not-so-bright Tom, gives him a punch in the shoulder. Then, everyone laughs at him.

Junior CRIES LOUDER now. Tom gives Susan an irritated look.

The crowd starts to break up. Billy stands and shakes hands with everyone.

MAN #1: Good to see you again, Bill.

Susan puts the baby up to her shoulder. He SPITS UP on Billy's Army jacket. She jumps up from the chair. Tom and Billy try to rescue the jacket. Angela grabs it first.

TOM: Jesus Christ, Susan, look at what the hell you've done.

SUSAN: I've been trying to get your ass out of here for two hours. He needs to go home.

Tom grabs Susan by the arm, fuming.

TOM: Nothin' stoppin' you from leaving. *(to Billy)* Billy, I'm sorry man.

Billy calms him down.

51

BILLY: It's okay. Tom, it's okay. I'll take it to the cleaners.

Tom lets go of Susan, smiles at Billy. Angela tries wiping the jacket with a napkin. Billy takes the jacket from her.

BILLY: It's okay, Angela. Let's get out of here.

SUSAN: Sorry 'bout the jacket, Billy. It's good to see you, the two of you, together again.

Billy looks at Angela and smiles. Susan and Tom EXIT, with Junior, arguing.

Billy exchanges an uncomfortable glance with Angela. He sits back down, looks around at the place, somewhat disappointed.

BILLY: Yeah, it's good... to be home. Where you wanna go?

He pulls Angela onto his lap, kisses her.

ANGELA: I got paid today. I have enough for a room.

Angela stands up, pulling Billy with her. He helps her on with her jacket. Billy takes a last drink of beer, looks around the room, looks at Hank, and throws a tip on the table. Hank trips over a chair, looking at Billy.

BILLY: What are we waitin' for then?

Billy EXITS ahead of Angela.

ANGELA: (*to herself*) You, Billy. I've been waitin' for you.

INT. MOTEL ROOM - NIGHT

Typical cheap motel room, same tired look as the rest of the town. Billy and Angela, stand, kissing, stumbling, taking off clothes, making their way to the bed. They tumble onto the bed. Billy on top of Angela, kissing her.

BILLY: You're still on the pill, right?

ANGELA: No, I'm not on the pill.

He stops kissing her, concerned.

ANGELA: It made me too sick.

Billy backs off. She pulls him back on, smiles.

ANGELA: Don't worry, I've got something. Freebies from the health clinic.

BILLY: Do you have to go do your thing? In the bathroom?

She kisses him.

ANGELA: Are you kidding? It's been in for hours.

He looks at her for a minute, loosens up again. They kiss.

ANGELA: I'm so glad you're comin' back home, Billy. Goin' into the Guard and all. I've missed you.

Billy hugs her.

BILLY: Yeah, back in good ol' Everly.

I/E. THE ONLY STOPLIGHT IN EVERLY – DAY

Angela sits in her HEAP OF A CAR, waiting on the red light to change. No other cars at the intersection. Angela taps her fingers on the dash.

The light seems stuck. Angela glances at the Cafe and Hardware Stores with going-out-of-business signs in their windows. AN ELDERLY MAN and WOMAN go into the hardware store.

Angela looks back at light. She waits. A pickup truck rolls through the intersection. She checks her watch. The light turns green. She moves on.

INT. DAIRY QUEEN - DAY

Angela, wearing her BLUE SMOCK and standard attire, ENTERS the restaurant. She spots Billy, Tom, Susan and Junior in a booth in the back. She notices a couple of high school GIRLS, 16, in a corner, looking Billy's way. She walks by.

The girls stop whispering as Angela walks by. Angela stops and turns to them.

ANGELA: Find your own ticket out of Everly, this one's already been stamped and comin' back home.

The Girls roll their eyes and turn away. Angela walks on to Billy's table.

TOM: Look, it's the lost smurf.

Angela slides in beside Billy. He pulls her close and gives her a kiss. Tom stuffs his face with a burger. Susan is trying to feed the baby. Angela gives Junior a kiss on the cheek.

ANGELA: How's my baby doin'? I'm gonna' get you.

Angela plays peek-a-boo with the baby. The baby grins at her. Billy pulls her away from the baby.

BILLY: I don't know about that one, but this one could use some attention.

TOM: Yeah, he's only got one more week here.

SILENCE. Billy throws a napkin at Tom, still eating his burger. Susan and Angela stare at each other.

ANGELA: What do you mean, you only got one more week? I thought your training was over.

Billy admonishes Tom with a stare. Angela looks at Billy for an answer. Tom wipes his mouth with the napkin and scoots out.

TOM: We better go, Suze. Let these lovebirds do some catching up.

SUSAN: No, I want to...

Tom scoots Susan out of the booth. He grabs Junior and the diaper bag, heads for the door.

TOM: Thanks for lunch, Bill. We'll be at the Parlor tonight.

Susan taps Angela on the arm.

SUSAN: This must be serious if Tom's helping me out. Call me.

Susan walks off. Billy puts his arm around Angela.

BILLY: Let's drive up to the lake.

Angela's eyes well up with tears. She knows something is up if he wants to drive to the lake.

EXT. LAKE - DAY

The leaves are almost off the trees, but it's a nice day. Empty beer cans are strewn along the edge of the lake, marking it as a local party spot.

Billy and Angela sit on a blanket, overlooking the lake, with a cooler beside them. Billy's used, but nice, sporty car is parked behind them. Angela is wrapped in another blanket, dabbing her eyes with its edge.

BILLY: Well, I see some things never change around here. Still drink the same damn beer.

Billy scoots closer to the edge of the bank, rubbing his temples. He reaches into the cooler and grabs a Coke, pops the tab off, and throws it into the lake. He offers Angela a drink, she shakes her head no.

ANGELA: When were you going to tell me, Billy? After you'd left?

BILLY: Damn, I am telling you. Right now.

ANGELA: (*yelling*) Yeah, after Tom slipped up.

BILLY: I was just waitin' for the right time...My drill sergeant picked me for active duty, said I was a natural, Ange.

ANGELA: Yeah? And I'm a clean-aisle-one natural. The hero's an even bigger hero in the Army.

Angela throws the blanket off.

ANGELA: That's all I've heard since you got back home, football and the Army. What about us?

Billy scoots back to Angela.

BILLY: Well, you sure don't want to hear about the Army now.

ANGELA: You said one year. Then we'd get...

He rubs her hands.

BILLY: I know, I know, Ang. I do love you.

ANGELA: I've waited here for you, Billy. Things haven't changed for me.

BILLY: I just want to save up some money. I can make more there than I can back here.

He pulls Angela closer to him. She resists.

BILLY: All the guys I've talked to said they save a lot in Korea. You can get stuff real cheap.

He hugs her and starts kissing her ear.

BILLY: How about a designer pocketbook, Ange? Or Nikes? They're real cheap there. You like Nikes.

Angela kisses him back. Things heat up between them.

ANGELA: You know, I could go with you, maybe. To Korea.

BILLY: No, I have to live in the barracks.

Billy is oblivious to what Angela is hinting at.

ANGELA: If we were married?

Billy pulls away.

BILLY: Damn, Angela. I can't afford both of us over there.

ANGELA: Thought you said it was cheap.

BILLY: Yeah, like stuff, Nikes and crap. Not living there.

Billy jumps up, pulls Angela up with him.

BILLY: I'll have 30 days leave in May.

ANGELA: Leave for where? You have to leave for someplace else?

Billy grins at her lack of knowledge.

BILLY: That's Army talk for vacation days. Maybe May. You don't want an ugly November wedding do you?

This seems to pacify Angela for the moment.

BILLY: Come on, let's go get our favorite room. I'll splurge for the whole week, Ange, Angel.

He lifts her chin.

BILLY: I couldn't have made it through Basic, without knowing you were here, waitin' for me.

INT. MOTEL ROOM - NIGHT

Angela and Billy are in bed, making out. Though Angela is not as passionate as before. This is pretty much the same routine while Billy is back in Everly.

INT. MOTEL BATHROOM - DAY

Angela gets dressed for work. Her eyes are swollen from crying. She tries to put on make-up to cover it up. She puts on her BLUE SMOCK. She looks in the mirror and frowns at the reflection staring back.

Angela tiptoes INTO THE BEDROOM and looks at Billy, who is asleep. She leans over and kisses him, then leaves.

EXT. SHOPS IN JEFFERSON - DAY

Jefferson is booming compared to Everly. A huge, old two-story converted house with a garage houses numerous shops. The SIGN says it houses MEDICAL OFFICES, a DRY CLEANERS, an ARMY/NAVY RECRUITING STATION, and a BEAUTY SHOP.

Angela pulls her heap that passes for a car into the parking lot. She backs her car into a slot near the road, gets out, CARRYING BILLY'S JACKET. She ENTERS the building. TIME PASSES

EXT. SHOPS IN JEFFERSON - DAY

A few PEOPLE, various ages, men and women, ENTER the building.

Angela EXITS the building, carrying a small BROWN PAPER BAG. She looks around, like she doesn't want to be seen. She gets into her car and throws the bag beside her BLUE SMOCK, and starts her car. It sputters, she pounds the dashboard.

INT. STORE - DAY

Angela and Susan stock some toothpaste on the shelves. CHUCKIE, 15, a pimply-faced stock boy, pushes a cart down the aisle. Same old same old for Angela, tedious work. Angela checks her watch.

CHUCKIE: Here, Mr. Vinson said you could stock this after you finished here.

He cuts open a box, embarrassed at the sight of tampons. Angela smiles as she put the last toothpaste on the shelf.

ANGELA: Here, I'll take care of them.

Chuck hurries away. Angela shakes her head. Susan walks over to see what's in the box. The INTERCOM SQUELCHES. Angela covers her ears with her hands.

MR. VINSON (OS): *(over intercom)* Tampons, tampons in aisle seven, need to be put in their proper place, A-SAP.

SUSAN: Oh, my God! Here, you go first.

Susan tosses one to Angela. They throw tampons at each other, LAUGHING hysterically. TWO OLDER LADIES, 60s, pushing a cart, shake their heads, and move to the next aisle

INT. PIZZA PARLOR - NIGHT

This night is pretty much the same as the last night at the Pizza Parlor. Billy sits with his group of GUYS, including Tom and Kevin. He's not in uniform this time. He's wearing his high school letterman's jacket this time. Hank has become part of the inner circle also.

BY THE JUKEBOX, Angela and Susan hang out with Junior again. Angela makes a selection on the jukebox.

SUSAN: Well, is it everything you hoped it would be, with Billy?

Angela looks at Billy, not sure.

ANGELA: Oh sure, Billy's great.

SUSAN: May isn't that far off.

Angela still stares at Billy. He looks at her.

ANGELA: No, not that far away.

SUSAN: Damn him, asking you to wait again.

Susan is very upset tonight. Angela looks at Susan.

ANGELA: He wants to save up...

SUSAN: I know, I know. Save up some more money. Just how much damned money does it take to come back here?

Susan starts to cry.

SUSAN: Or get married? My wedding only cost fifteen dollars. Shit!

Susan shakes. Angela takes Junior. Susan RUNS OUT of the parlor. Angela meets Billy's gaze for a second, bouncing the baby on her hip.

Billy turns back to the guys. Angela walks TO BILLY'S TABLE.

Angela hands Junior to him, looks at Tom who is busy stuffing his face with pizza. Billy is caught off guard.

BILLY: Angela.

ANGELA: Just hold him for a minute. It won't kill you.

Billy, uncomfortably, bounces the baby on his lap. Angela turns away and walks outside.

EXT. PARKING LOT - NIGHT

Susan sits on the hood of her car, drinking a beer, crying. She puts her head in her hands. Angie walks over to Susan, rubs her back.

SUSAN: I'm just so tired...he never helps out.

Susan looks up at Angela.

SUSAN: Do you really want to be part of the P-B-20 club, Angela?

ANGELA: P-what?

Susan jumps off the car, picks up some gravel and starts throwing them at her car.

SUSAN: Pregnant before 20 club. Yeah, you can join me...

She throws a rock for each name she calls out.

SUSAN: Janice, Christy, Maggie, Joanna...

Angela stops her, and soothes her back to reality.

ANGELA: Let me take Junior tonight.

Susan straightens up, wipes her eyes.

SUSAN: No, you need to spend time with Billy. I'll take him to Mama's. At least I have her.

Angela turns away at the mention of a mother.

SUSAN: I'm sorry, Ang. I know you've had to take care of Jenny... and your mother.

ANGELA: I guess my Mom was a founding member of the club, huh?

Angela and Susan hug and trip over each other, landing on the ground. They roll onto

59

their backs, laughing.

ANGELA: Who in the hell came up with the B-P...

SUSAN: No, no, it's P-B 20. Pregnant before. I came up with it. Hell, they have their club, why can't we have ours?

They pick up some gravel and start hitting the Pizza Parlor sign.

ANGELA: Yeah, why can't we. I'll start the A-W-O-T. The A-Wot Club.

Susan turns to Angela.

SUSAN: What the hell is that?

ANGELA: The Always Waiting on Them Club.

Susan and Angela look at each other, LAUGHING.

SUSAN: Hey...wot. Wot you lookin' at?

A LADY, 40s, walks through the parking lot, hanging onto a MAN, 50s, shaking her head.

ANGELA: *(failed Italian accent)* Hey, what-about-it club.

Susan and Angela sit up, LAUGHING through the hurt, until their sides ache.

EXT. SHOPS IN JEFFERSON - DAY

Angela pulls her car into the parking lot, backing it up as usual, facing the road. She sits in her car for a minute. She looks back at the building.

VARIOUS PEOPLE, *one MAN in Navy uniform, some WOMEN, mostly older, tired women or young tired-looking women, various ages, walk IN and OUT of the door. Some have been to the beauty parlor, with freshly done hairdos.*

Angela reaches down onto the floorboard and GRABS the BROWN PAPER BAG, beside her BLUE SMOCK. She gets out of the car and ENTERS the building. TIME PASSES.

Angela EXITS the building, with PAPERS in one hand and BILLY'S JACKET in the other. She hurries to her car. She starts it up, it sputters.

ANGELA: Shit!

She pounds the dashboard, it starts up. She pulls out.

INT. ANGELA'S BEDROOM - DAY

Angela's rummaging through her closet like a mad woman, crying. She grabs the shoebox she's looking for, pulls out a pair of Nike running shoes, circa 1980s. She rips off the small pom-poms on them. She grabs a sweat suit in the bottom of her closet. She HEARS someone stumbling around.

LINDA (O.S.): Angie, is that you?

She looks around the room like a trapped animal. She runs to the window with no screen in it, takes off her high heels, opens the window, and climbs out.

LINDA (O.S.): I want to talk to you. Angela!

Through window, we see Angela running to her car, parked at the rear of her house.

EXT. LAKE - DAY

MONTAGE OF ANGELA RUNNING

Angela pulls her car into a clearing by the lake. She struggles to change into her sweat suit.

She gets out of her car and puts on her running shoes. She stretches and takes off running.

Angela runs on the road by the lake, uphill, barely making it. She is BREATHING HARD, sweating. She slows, alternating between a walk, run, walk, run. She runs steady again, making it to the top.

Various shots of her running and walking.

Angela runs downhill, her car in view. She stops when she reaches her car, holding her side, covered in sweat, crying, and uneven breathing. Angela opens her car door, leans by it. She gets sick and we HEAR her throwing up.

Angela climbs into her car, calming down. She sits very still.

A car pulls into the other end of the clearing near Angela's car. Angela watches them.

A TEENAGE BOY #1 and GIRL #1 get out of the car, carrying blankets and a six-pack of beer, hanging onto each other. It's getting dark. Angela watches them walk out of site, down the bank.

END OF MONTAGE

INT. TOM'S TRAILER - NIGHT

Tom's trailer is a mess. Dishes in sink, baby bottles all over the counter. Junior CRIES in the background, off screen.

Billy sits with Tom and Kevin, playing cards and drinking beer at the kitchen table. Tom wears a SANITATION COMPANY UNIFORM. Billy wears his ARMY PT UNIFORM. Kevin wears a MECHANIC'S SHIRT.

TOM: Susan!

Tom shuffles his cards around.

TOM: Yeah, this has been the best damn thing that's happened to Me. settled me down. You'll handle it, if Angela's...

KEVIN: Yeah, you're handling it, ain't ya'?

TOM: Well, Ange has been over here enough. She knows how to handle the kid. Susan!

Junior CRIES louder. Billy shuffles his cards around, trying to ignore Tom. Kevin, agitated, throws his cards down onto the table.

TOM: What the hell are you doin'?

KEVIN: She went to work, asshole. She told you yesterday she was taking a double shift today.

TOM: Glad someone listens to her. Maybe you should have married her then.

Billy and Kevin look at each other. Tom keeps his eyes on his cards. Kevin jumps up to check on the baby in the next room.

BILLY: Look, Angela was just gettin' some birth control.

Tom tosses a card in the pile. He grins, looking at Billy.

TOM: In Jefferson? You know those are real doctors over there. And they ain't free.

Billy looks up at Tom. An understanding passes between them.

TOM: Whatever you say, Billy boy. I just' know she's been waitin' for you to come home.

Tom picks up a card and studies his hand.

TOM: Women get crazy ideas. You're off to Korea. She had plans that got scrapped because her Mom went to jail for a few months.

Tom lays his cards on the table.

TOM: How do you think I got in this mess? Susan knew I was goin' to Ohio, to work for my uncle.

Billy fidgets in his chair, feeling the walls closing in around him. Junior is still crying. Billy checks his watch, stands up, puts his cards down.

BILLY: Well, Tom...

TOM: It's good to let 'em cry for awhile. Remember that, Billy.

BILLY: I'll remember, Tom. I gotta' go.

INT. MOTEL ROOM - DAY

Billy comes tearing into the room. He looks around, goes INTO BATHROOM.

Billy goes through the bathroom cabinet, searching for something. He spots Angela's overnight bag, under the sink.

He dumps its contents onto the floor. Everything falls out, including a MEDICAL URINE SAMPLE CUP. He sits on the floor, holding the cup, dazed. He punches the floor with his fist.

BILLY: Shit! Damn it!

He crams the contents back into the bag.

INT. MOTEL ROOM - NIGHT

Angela and Billy are lying on the bed. They stare at the ceiling.

ANGELA: Don't you want me, Billy?

BILLY: Yes, Angela. I'm just tired. You know, I ran 10 miles today. I still have to keep in shape.

Billy turns over to Angela. She looks at him.

BILLY: Are you sure there's nothin' you want to talk about, Angela.

ANGELA: Would you stop givin' me the third degree? Why you actin' so strange tonight?

Angela looks away. Billy gets up and grabs some money off the table. He sighs.

BILLY: Just want to know if... you need money or anything... I know your mom...

Angela stands up, walks to the window.

ANGELA: My mom what?

BILLY: I know she makes you pay your own way. If you need money for something, tell me, okay?

ANGELA: No, Billy, I don't need your money.

Billy walks over to Angela, rubs her shoulders.

ANGELA: Trust me, Linda makes plenty of money doing what she does.

BILLY: Let's go get a pizza. Then, we'll come back, okay? I've only got a couple more days.

ANGELA: You go, I'll wait here for you.

He gives her a kiss and EXITS. Angela pulls a curtain back and watches him pull out.

EXT. TOWN OF EVERLY - SUNRISE

A shot of the town of Everly, nothing much going on. Many businesses sit empty.

INT. BILLY'S CAR - DAY

Billy and Angela sit in the store's parking lot. His nice car sits beside her heap of a car.

Angela watches WOMEN, mostly young, tug their YOUNG CHILDREN in and out of the store, or older LADIES, 60s, the blue-hair rinse crowd.

BILLY: I was able to buy this with my bonus. I've got a little work to do on it.

Billy runs his hands over the steering wheel of his car.

ANGELA: Now it's cars and football? You've been here two weeks...

BILLY: No, Angela. The guys like that talkin' football. Back here, they're still living their glory days.

Angela looks at Billy, ready to let him have it.

ANGELA: Listen to you. Like you've been somewhere.

BILLY: Well, the Army is somewhere and... it changes things.

ANGELA: Yeah, the old gang's living their glory days. Shit.

Angela looks out the window.

ANGELA: Tom's driving 60 miles a day to work for his cousin in the garbage business. Susan works her ass off at work...

Angela bangs her fist on the dashboard.

ANGELA: And at home because Tom doesn't do shit to help her. Kevin has permanent grease marks under his nails. And me?

Angela stares at the store. A BOY, 17, gathers up shopping carts.

ANGELA: I drive 20 miles for a crappy job, in a crappy car, and take one college class at a time. Just maybe I'll graduate by 40... I'm takin' crap off Linda...

She looks back at Billy.

ANGELA: And I'm here waiting for you to come home.

BILLY: Well, you just summed it up, Ange. Nothing here for me to come back to.

Angela attempts to get out of the car. Billy pulls her back.

BILLY: I didn't mean you... I couldn't make it in college, Angela.

He lets her go and stares straight ahead.

BILLY: I lied.

Angela looks at Billy, waiting for the big one.

ANGELA: What do you mean, you lied?

BILLY: I lied about college. I quit the team. They didn't take my scholarship away.

Angela, stunned, tries to process this information.

BILLY: They would've taken it. I quit goin' to practice. I quit goin' to class.

Billy takes Angela's hand, looks at her.

BILLY: I didn't want to play football anymore. And I wasn't interested, smart enough for college, Ange.

ANGELA: Why didn't you come back and get a job then?

BILLY: I couldn't face the guys... I couldn't let them know it was my fault. And you... knowin' you should have been there instead.

Billy searches Angela's eyes for some understanding.

BILLY: This fits me. That's why I'm going active, Angela. I don't want to come back here, go in the Guard or farm.

Billy looks up at the store.

Angela watches a TEENAGE BOY #2 and TEENAGE GIRL #2, about 17, try to put a fussy TODDLER into his car seat, in the car next to them. They could be a carbon copy of Billy and Angela, minus the child.

Teenage Boy #2 gets agitated. They argue with each other. He gets into the drivers' side, leaving the Teenage Girl #2 to wrestle with the kid.

BILLY: I'll be able to save more money in Korea. I get extra pay over there.

Angela looks at Billy, looks at his new car stereo, runs her fingers over it.

ANGELA: Yeah, I can see how you've saved some money for us.

She opens the door. He leans to kiss her. She kisses him, without her usual zest.

ANGELA: I couldn't just leave Jenny here alone, with Mom and her drug arrest.

BILLY: Angela, you don't owe your Mom nothing. She owes you for always being here to pick up her pieces.

Angela turns away and watches the Teenage Girl #2 finally strap the Toddler into his car seat. The Girl #2 and Angela exchange glances. She gets into the car, slamming the door shut.

BILLY: Want me to pick you up at seven? Don't tell the guys, about the bum I've been, okay?

ANGELA: Sure, Billy. I'll be waitin' for you.

Angela gets out of Billy's car, watching as the couple's car pulls out of the parking lot. Billy watches Angela walk away.

INT. RESTROOM AT THE STORE - DAY

Angela opens the stall doors to the toilets. One is really nasty, overflowing. She grimaces and almost barfs. She shuts the door. She rolls the bucket of water and mop over to the stalls.

Angela is down on the floor scrubbing one of the toilets.

She marks her initials, A-S-T, on a form stuck to the bathroom door. She looks at it a second and then erases the T and puts a J.

Angela walks to the sink, turns the faucet on, and pumps the soap dispenser. She scrubs her hands, looking at her disheveled self in the mirror. She can't get any lower than this.

She tries to pull a paper towel out of the dispenser. It's out.

ANGELA: Shit!

She opens the restroom door.

INT. STORE'S STOCK ROOM - DAY

Angela turns on a light and searches the shelves for paper towels. DUFF MURPHY, 30, enters the room. He's wears a store vest, tight jeans and cowboy boots.

He sneaks up behind Angela. She jumps, dropping the napkins.

ANGELA: Duff, what the hell you doin'? Sneakin' up on a girl like that?

Duff invades her space, she pulls back.

DUFF: You didn't seem to mind it last month. So, heard Billy boy's goin' to Korea. Let me know if he's not man enough for you.

Angela pulls away from him.

DUFF: So, we can start riding to work together.

Angela, confused, looks at Duff.

ANGELA: What are you talkin' about?

DUFF: Your Mama's gonna come keep house for me. She didn't tell you yet?

She pushes by Duff and opens the door. He laughs.

DUFF: Plenty of room for you, Angela.

A very mad Angela walks out of the stock room.

INT. ANGELA'S HOUSE - EVENING

Angela bursts through the door. She's in a panic, looking for Jenny. She opens Jenny's bedroom door and stands in JENNY'S DOORWAY.

Her child's room is empty. The closet doors hang off the hinge. Her clothes are gone. Her bed covers are gone. A couple of stuffed animals are on the floor.

ANGELA: Mom... mama?!

Angela sees a glow of light from her Mother's bedroom. She opens the door INTO LINDA'S BEDROOM.

Linda is lying on the bed, watching a TV soap opera without the sound, smoking a cigarette.

ANGELA: Where's Jenny?

LINDA: Don't have a cow. She's with Grandma.

Linda snuffs out her cigarette in an ashtray. She stares at the TV.

LINDA: Guess you've seen Duff.

ANGELA: Yeah, I've seen Duff.

Angela calms down some. Linda sits on the side of the bed.

LINDA: I can't pay the rent on this place anymore.

ANGELA: So what caused this big change of heart for Duff?

LINDA: Besides him kicking out Amy? Miss Edna saw you at the G-Y-N, over in Jefferson, the other day. And I ain't staying around here...

Linda gets up and starts grabbing clothes and stuffing them into a suitcase.

ANGELA: Is that all you think I'm capable of? Gettin' pregnant? That's your department, not mine.

Linda turns around and SLAPS Angela. Angela rubs her face, tears well up.

LINDA: Oh, baby. I'm so sorry.

Linda hugs Angela. She pulls away and cries.

ANGELA: I can get a second job... quit my college class.

Linda holds Angela by the arms and looks at her, as if seeing her for the first time.

LINDA: Baby, don't you quit your classes. You have a good head. Don't waste it on that boy, or me.

Linda rubs Angela's cheek.

LINDA: Duff ain't much, but I need a change. He lives in another county. Maybe, I can get myself together there...

Angela sits down on the bed.

ANGELA: Grandma can't...

LINDA: Jenny likes it better at Grandma's.

Linda looks around her room.

LINDA: Can't say I blame her. Grandma said you can stay there, too.

She picks up her suitcase, stands in the doorway.

LINDA: We have to be out of here by Wednesday.

Angela looks at her, crying. Linda turns to leave, throws the keys to Angela. Angela catches them.

LINDA: Just leave the keys here. I guess I can call the Turners to find you after Wednesday.

Linda hesitates.

LINDA: Don't make the same mistake I made, baby. Havin' kids too young and when I didn't need them.

Linda walks out. Angela lies back on the bed, puts pillow over her face and cries like a

69

baby.

EXT. SHOPS IN JEFFERSON - DAY

Angela, in a rush, pulls her car into the parking lot. This time she pulls in, so she faces the building. She sits and looks at the building. TIME PASSES.

Angela takes some PAPERS from her glove compartment and gets out of the car. She ENTERS the building.

INT. DOCTOR'S WAITING ROOM

Angela sits in the waiting room, with paperwork on a clipboard. A BABY crawls over to Angela. She smiles at the baby. The MOTHER, 20s, picks the baby up. OTHER WOMEN, various ages, some with SMALL CHILDREN wait also.

RECEPTIONIST (O.S.): Miss Jacobs.

Angela, nervous, takes the paperwork up to the counter. The RECEPTIONIST, 40s, takes it, checking it over.

ANGELA: Do you see many... of these in here?

Receptionist makes a mark on the papers.

RECEPTIONIST: Oh, not for a while. Not seen too many women make this choice.

The Receptionist looks up at Angela

RECEPTIONIST: But hon, if I were your age, I'd be doing the same thing.

She hands Angela a pen.

ANGELA: Where do I sign?

RECEPTIONIST: Here, you need to sign right here. And here's a copy for you to take to them. They're out to lunch right now. Catch them in after one.

Angela hesitates, then signs and takes the copy. The Receptionist pats her hand.

RECEPTIONIST: Good luck. Just be sure this is what you wanna do. There'll be no takin' it back.

Angela breathes a sigh of thanks. She leaves the office.

EXT. PARKING LOT - DAY

Angela walks across the parking lot, gets INTO HER HEAP OF A CAR.

Angela starts to hyperventilate. She rolls the window down. She picks up her BLUE SMOCK, puts it on. She backs out, turns her car around. She glances into the rearview mirror at the office sign.

ANGELA: I'm doing the right thing...I am.

She pulls out onto the road.

EXT. STORE PARKING LOT - NIGHT

Billy pulls into the parking lot, driving around looking for Angela's car. He checks his watch. He pulls out.

EXT. TOWN OF EVERLY - NIGHT

Billy drives through town. A few cars here and there. He drives by Angela's house. Billy drives by the Pizza Parlor. TEENAGERS congregate in the parking lot of the Parlor, sitting on the tailgates of pick-up trucks. No sign of Angela. They wave to Billy.

INT. MOTEL ROOM - NIGHT

Billy watches television. He walks to the window and looks out. He picks up the telephone and dials, hangs up. He grabs his jacket and heads out the door.

EXT. LOU'S GAS STATION - BEFORE DAWN

Angela, dressed in her jeans, heels, sweater and BLUE SMOCK, talks on the pay phone, crying.

ANGELA: I just need to see you right now, Billy. Please. I'm at Lou's, I can be right there.

INT. BILLY'S BEDROOM - BEFORE DAWN

Billy's house is modest, but nicer than Angela's house. His room is full of football trophies, pictures of Angela and an Army recruiting poster.

Billy is dressed in hunting clothes. He stands, picking lint off his dress Army uniform, with phone in his hand.

BILLY: I'm going huntin' in half an hour with Grandpa and his buddies. Can't it wait until after I get back home...Okay, okay, calm down. Be here in five minutes.

EXT. LOU'S GAS STATION - BEFORE DAWN

Angela hangs up the phone. She wipes her eyes, stuffs some PAPERS into her pocket. She gets into

INT. ANGELA'S CAR

Angela tries to start the car.

ANGELA: Shit!

She pounds the dashboard. It sputters, then starts up. She pulls out, drives through the town.

INT. ANGELA'S CAR IN EVERLY- BEFORE DAWN

Angela stops at the one and only stoplight. No traffic, again. Angela watches a GUY stumble out of the Pool Hall. She strums her fingers on the steering wheel.

Light seems stuck on red. Angela revs up her car and SLAMS on the gas. She runs the red light.

EXT. BILLY'S STREET - NIGHT

Angela pulls onto Billy's street. The car starts to sputter and it jerks to its final resting place by the curb.

Angela gets out of the car, kicks its tire. She looks down the street and sees one porch light on. She sees a figure sitting on the porch swing.

EXT. BILLY'S HOUSE - BEFORE DAWN

Billy sits outside on the porch swing waiting for Angela. He twists his Army BDU cap in his hand.

BILLY: *(to himself)* Now, look Angela. I can't take you to Korea with me, even if you are pr...

He stands up.

BILLY: It's like this. I don't want to be tied... I think we need a break.

Billy HEARS CLICKING ON the sidewalk. He turns to look behind him. It's Angela. Billy stands up and sits on the steps. Angela sits down beside him.

ANGELA: Everyone still in bed?

BILLY: Grandpa's up getting ready.

Angela's eyes are red from crying. She stares straight ahead, with her hands in her smock's pockets.

Billy glances at her, down at his cap. He checks his watch.

BILLY: What couldn't wait until this afternoon?

Angela takes a deep breath.

ANGELA: I've been doing a lot of thinking since you got back, Billy. Wanting me to wait some more for you...

BILLY: Angela.

Billy looks like he's about to lose it. He looks at Angela. She turns to him.

ANGELA: I've watched Susan, how hard it's been for her. And, I think you don't want to be with me no more.

BILLY: Now, Ange...

ANGELA: Just let me finish, Billy.

He looks away.

ANGELA: I just thought we'd always be together. I don't know how to tell you this.

Irritated, Billy throws his cap down and stands up.

BILLY: Damn. Let's get it over with.

Angela takes the PAPERS out of her pocket, unfolds them, stands up and HANDS THEM TO Billy.

ANGELA: Here, just take a look at these for me. Make sure I didn't sign up for anything too crazy.

Billy takes them and moves under the street light. He sees they are ARMY ENLISTMENT PAPERS. His face has a look of confusion, not what he expected. Angela dabs her eyes with a tissue.

BILLY: Ange... I....

ANGELA: Just don't tell me I'm stupid. My mother does that enough. She won't miss me... But Jenny, I don't know how to tell her. She'll be okay, won't she, Billy?

A PAPERBOY, 10, rides by and tosses a newspaper. Billy is still stunned.

PAPERBOY: Hey, Billy.

Billy ignores him.

BILLY: I see what you're doing. This doesn't mean you'll go to Korea, Angie. I'll be on the D-M-Z.

He paces back and forth underneath the light.

BILLY: And you'll be far south of there. If you even got there at all.

Angela GRABS the enlistment papers from Billy.

ANGELA: I don't need a geography lesson, Billy. And this ain't about you. This is about me.

Angela looks at Billy for some recognition of understanding.

ANGELA: *(rambling)* Look, I know I only made cheerleader because we were dating. Hell, I wanted to just run track, but I quit for you. And, I got that job because of your Aunt.

BILLY: I don't...

ANGELA: I'll even go in as an E-2, Private. Because of my college credits.

Billy turns away from Angela. He is stunned, even looks about to cry. He turns back to Angela.

BILLY: Angela, the Army's no place for a woman.

ANGELA: Neither is this place.

She opens her arms wide, with the papers in her hand, referring to Everly.

ANGELA: Don't you get it? I don't want to end up like Susan, like my Mother. I just want... out. On my terms.

Billy takes her hands in his. He pulls her to him.

Angela gives Billy a big, final hug, like she will never see him again, then let's go. Billy

74

dabs at the tears in his eyes.

ANGELA: You better go meet your Grandpa. I'll be seein' ya, Billy.

Angela stuffs the PAPERS back into her jeans pocket and walks away.

A stunned Billy watches her walk down the street. The screen door SLAMS. His GRANDPA, 60s, walks onto the porch. Billy continues to watch Angela walk down the street.

EXT. STREET IN EVERLY - DAWN

Angela continues walking down the street, with tears of relief now, wiping her eyes with a tissue.

Angela stops by her broken down car, takes off her SMOCK and throws it inside. She grabs her NIKE RUNNING SHOES.

Angela THROWS HER HIGH HEELS down the street and puts on her Nikes. She laughs and starts walking through the empty town.

ANGELA BREAKS INTO A RUN through Everly.

FADE OUT:

5 ON BECOMING AN INDEPENDENT FILM

My name is on the script whenever it gets made. I take the blame... one of my crusades is to defend the writer because the script is the basis of the whole thing... every good director knows that... not that she (the director) isn't probably the most important member of the team, but the picture can't be made without the many other talents...

- Eleanor Perry

I sit at my computer, alone and in the dark, at our home in Alabama. We'd moved in 2004, and it is now 2005. It's early morning, and I've even risen earlier than my Army husband, before his 5 a.m. wake-up call. I open an email and scream. My daughter and husband both run into my home office.

"What's wrong?" Both of them in unison say.

I am overcome with emotion, barely able to speak. Tears bubble up, as well as a lump in my throat.

"Nothing... I have a theme song."

"A what?"

"Mat sent me the theme song. To *Angela's Decision*."

I begin playing it again on the computer.

"Mom, that's great."

While they didn't enjoy the too-early alarm, nearly scaring them to death, they both congratulated me, and then went back to bed. Me? I played and replayed it, over and over again, the song written by Liam Gerner from the film that was still in the making. Mat King, the director, would keep me in the loop during the entire filmmaking process of *Angela's Decision* being filmed in Australia in February 2006, via email, and I would forever hold him as the gold standard of how a director and producer should treat a screenwriter. My experience of trying to seal a deal on an option at the time with a cable network would not go as smoothly.

After defending my thesis in July 2003, with my husband just returned from Iraq (and also sitting in a nearby office while I defended my thesis in a conference room at OU), and after making several trips later in the year to OU to make sure my thesis was safely placed in the Bizzell Memorial Library, we would receive orders for assignment to Huntsville, Alabama. I would jokingly refer to Alabama as LA backwards (AL, get it?), a joke that only my daughter would appreciate. I would eventually find a great film community in northern Alabama and even experience being on film sets for the first time to see how a film is put together and how all the pieces and crew fit. That would become invaluable to me as a writer.

This would be a strange time, as I was in negotiations for an option for the holiday feature screenplay from my graduate thesis with a cable network and Canadian producer. I had pitched this script at The Screenwriting Conference in Santa Fe, along with *Angela's Decision* as a television pilot script. One of the producers wanted the holiday romcom.

While I didn't really focus on *Angela* at the conference in 2003, I did pitch it to a Showtime executive as a potential TV script. She was intrigued with my idea and interested in turning it into a series. Keep in mind women in the Army were in the news. Jessica Lynch had been rescued, and the debate still raged on about women even being in the Army, let alone Iraq (Afghanistan was losing ground in more ways than one). Iraq wasn't even a year into the war, but the nature of the war had changed. The executive from Showtime took the script to LA. But a couple of months later, I'd learn she was let go, and all her projects as well – a common practice, it seemed, in Hollywood.

Alabama was not an easy place for me, in the beginning. We had a contentious election year in 2004, and the war in Iraq was at the forefront of debates. Oklahoma had been full of soldiers and families who had gone through the first massive deployments, unlike the Alabama Army town. While OK had roughly 30,000 soldiers and family members, Alabama had less than one thousand soldiers and was made up of defense contractors and government civilians, also due to the NASA space center. The Army was big business here. Attitudes leaned towards the conservative, and it got ugly if you disagreed with the war, with the President, with just about anything. Even homes and cars reflected a pay scale not seen at larger Army posts like Fort Sill, where fifty percent of the kids at my daughter's junior high there had been on free or reduced lunch and most still had a parent deployed.

Mix that with the "for us or against us" mentality, and it was not an easy place to be. Even my mini-van, that same one I drove to take my husband to his deployment departure a year earlier, would be surrounded by a group of men, simply because I had a sticker on my van that reflected a differing choice for president – a right that I served for myself, not to mention my husband who was still serving. But I eventually found my small tribe in Alabama in the form of writers, artists, and filmmakers, and even a place to watch indie films at the Flying Monkey Arts Center.

I also found familiarity in writing a feature script adaptation of a book I'd picked up at a flea market. Though this novel was written a couple of hundred years ago and set in the 1600s, I thought it reflected the turmoil, political upheaval, and religious fervor of our present day (Mel Gibson's *The Passion Of The Christ* debuted then, to give even more context), to include the war in Iraq. Ago. The writer, Alexandre Dumas, was long deceased and the book in public domain, so I didn't need his permission to adapt.

Between that and my feature script negotiations, honestly, I forgot about *Angela's Decision*. But I did have experience adapting my own short story and that helped me feel capable of tackling a novel.

While many writers of short scripts direct their own scripts as well, I was not a director, and I had no desire to be, so after moving, I really didn't think much about *Angela's Decision*. I listed it on a website, Inktip.com, that links screenwriters and their scripts with directors and producers. Since I had listed a feature script, I could list a short for free, so I did. Listed and forgotten about.

The feature script talks had become a year-long negotiation in 2003 stretching into 2004. I had a teleconference with a high-powered actor's family member and the cable network's executive. They wanted a page-one rewrite (which meant I would rewrite the entire script from page one, which I was willing to do) before going to contract and various other things. Being new to this, I not only had an agent, but also secured an attorney from the California Lawyers for the Arts organization to help guide me through the seemingly irrational process.

Of course, I was willing to do the rewrite, take a smaller deal, and agree to other stipulations, but I was advised not to work without a contract at all and to hold out for a paid option, which would have been disadvantageous to any writer living in LA, let alone LA backwards. This deal could have helped me gain traction to becoming a WGA writer eventually, but the cable network chose to go through a company in Canada to option my script, so I would not gain WGA points at all. It was a lesson learned. (Also in 2004, the cable network executive wanted my other script loglines and I sent them in an email and phone call exchange – the one I was working on about a group of Army wives who would not otherwise be friends, thrown together by deployment and Army life, known tentatively as *War Torn*. Remember, we were in the throes of two wars at that time and

Hollywood took notice. Yes, a similar show eventually aired in 2006 for several seasons on that same network I had pitched to, and, no, I did not work on that show as a writer, etc. Yes, that was a tough pill to swallow, too, as I learned another lesson about doing business in LA, with some folks, anyway).

Moving on. Being a bit wiser and a bit worn down, but with at least a paid option in LA now, I reflected on what Suzanne Clauser, the screenwriter from the Antioch Writers Workshop in Ohio, had told me a decade earlier. With no chance of moving to LA, how in the world was I going to be a screenwriter, living in Alabama? A produced screenwriter, miles away from Hollywood?

Good things also come from emails. Mat King wanted to film *Angela's Decision* – in Australia. And not just film there, but also set Angela's story in Australia, complete with an Australian cast and crew.

My feature script deal provided a good training ground for future options and for the contract for *Angela's Decision*. I may not have been able to live in LA, but I knew I wanted to keep the rights to that story for future use. He agreed. I gave the rights to director Mat King to create a short film only from my script – keeping the rights to my screenplay, characters, and story for myself, which would allow me to write a feature, a TV series, or maybe even a novel or anything else. You can do this type of contract for a short film, however, it's very difficult to do with a feature. I did not want to keep those rights to my holiday script, and even though I was willing to hand over all rights to the production company, they still made the option negotiations an unnecessarily long ordeal. The deal with Mat would be smooth sailing, and the contract was signed immediately.

My thesis chair from OU, Andy Horton, had also featured me and my script *Angela's Decision* as one of several Oklahoma-based screenwriters in his article, *Five Easy Ways To Write Locally and Reach the World*, in *Screentalk* magazine. What he wrote about was about to come true in my case.

I wrote this script in Oklahoma, I had since moved to Alabama, and that script was about to become a globally-made film. This may sound commonplace now in the age of prolific social media outlets, but this was in 2005 -- before Facebook, Twitter, Instagram, and the rest, except for MySpace. MySpace was the only social media (other than the then-defunct Friendster), and filmmakers and musicians latched onto it for promotion. This was also the age of cell phones without camera-ready access and without unlimited data for one price. Roaming charges were in place, sometimes creating phone bills in the hundreds of dollars if you traveled and didn't understand that (yes, that happened on the trip my daughter and I took to New Mexico). AOL Instant Message, or AIM, was the untraditional way to communicate.

Mat had directed another short film that had been in festivals, and he also directed commercials, with many made in Vietnam and available to view online. He'd also worked on a feature and a TV show. While he perused my script, I viewed his commercials and short, and I had my fingers crossed. His storytelling ability, even in commercials, was visually superior to most. I had a great feeling about him making *Angela's Decision*.

I had not envisioned just how great of a job he would do. While we had signed an official contract in 2005, the shooting dates were pushed up to February 2006 due to his busy schedule and those of others involved in the film. This would help to cushion the blow of the holiday feature being optioned but not produced later on (the option lasted through mid-2006). With that option finalized at least, I was ready to move onto the filming of *Angela's Decision*, even from a world away.

When Mat told me he was in pre-production, I really didn't know what that meant (though I sure do now). What he did was put together a cast and crew that made a fifty-minute film in six days. Top level crew. From the cinematographer on down. They wanted to work with Mat. The two leads were cast. Xavier Samuel had done a couple of features. Rhiannon Owen was the perfect fit. She was Angela. Xavier was Billy, or Will rather (to reflect the Australian version). The two lead roles with these promising young actors could not have been cast any better, as well as the supporting actors in their roles.

The music itself was yet another adaptation of the story and screenplay. Not only had Mat adapted the script to be a film set in Australia with an Australian cast and crew, but he also tapped world class musicians, worlds away from him, to compose the twelve tracks of original music for the film.

Then London-based, Australian singer-songwriter Liam Gerner, who had toured with Elton John and Alanis Morissette, wrote a powerful theme song based solely on reading the script, before he even saw a cut of the film, along with seven more songs. Christopher Slaski, an award-winning composer based in Madrid but originally from London and a graduate of the Royal Academy of Music, who'd worked on a Kevin Spacey film, along with many foreign films and in theater, composed four tracks. One of Christopher's songs would go on to be a finalist in the Garden State Film Festival in New Jersey when the film would make film fest rounds in 2007.

While I didn't travel to Australia for the filming, as most writers are not on set, I literally watched the film unfold via email attachments. Mat sent me casting photos of actors that he was considering, and then when filming began in 2006, he would send me film stills from the actual film. Of course he had to make some changes to the script. He brought the story up to present day, and instead of Will (Billy) being assigned to Korea, he was assigned to Iraq. Mat asked me if I wanted to know if he had kept both ending, and I said no. The ending was important to me and to both

Angela's and Will's stories, and while I hoped he'd kept that intact, I really wanted to be surprised by watching the story unfold onscreen. I knew just by looking at the pictures that Mat sent to me that the story of Angela and Billy seemed to have varied very little and that in the filming process, Mat, the crew, and certainly the actors had captured something I could not even have imagined.

Mat would film *Angela's Decision* in six days, something I would learn later on after working on sets myself was an amazing feat. After quickly wrapping production by early March, *Angela's Decision* went into post-production, and I would check my email daily for updates. I was anxious to see the film, but I knew that the editing would take some time. (I had no idea what the true meaning of post-production entailed until a few years later when my then 16-year-old daughter would go to film school at Northwestern University in Evanston, IL, and I would watch her go through it for her own short films).

In September 2006, my daughter's junior year of high school, I received a rough cut of the film in the mail. She was home sick from school that day, and we watched together on the small screen on my laptop, as it could play PAL format, and our DVD player could not. So we sat in our darkened living room in Alabama and watched the story of Angela and Will unfold, as well as the stories of Susan, Tom, Angela's mom, Linda, and the setting also. Their stories had become everything I'd hoped it would be on film. The resemblance of the landscape of South Australia to where we had lived in southwest Oklahoma where I wrote the script was uncanny -- the open, barren landscape, the small towns surrounding it, the characters. Even the lone tree that Angela runs by in the opening scene mirrored one that I drove by every day when taking my daughter to school.

The changes to the script that were evident in the film were barely noticeable on my part. I couldn't even remember if I'd written a scene or if

Mat had changed it. Angela and Will's most intimate scene was definitely more detailed on screen, making more of an impact as a turning point in the story. Some scenes were consolidated and fit much better on film. Some were tweaked due to location. One scene in my script had Will and his friends playing poker at Tom's place. In the film, the guys are outside hitting golf balls instead, but with the same dialogue. I was so mesmerized by the transformation on screen that I had to go back to my own script to compare how I had even written it. Taking the scene from interior to exterior was seamless with the dialogue and had more of an impact.

Why make my script? When Mat and I spoke when he was first interested in the script, he said he had given the script a read with some friends at a local café. They had found the characters and setting very relatable to their own hometowns in Australia. In other words, they knew Angela and Billy from Everly, Oklahoma (and Everly, West Virginia from *Billy's Return*). Not only could they relate to the lack of good jobs, but also to the suffocating feeling of working dead-end jobs, especially when you are a young person looking at your life ahead of you. The sign of a great director, to further adapt the story and make it globally relatable.

I can't even describe my experience of first watching *Angela's Decision* with my teenage daughter. I recall laughter, tears, screams, silence, and then my "Oh my God" moment. Mat King really captured the faithfulness of the characters and story and made this gritty, heart wrenching drama come alive. No matter where it was set, it would resonate with people later on at festivals and screenings.

And Mat could not have put together a better team, to include an amazing cinematographer. Later in 2006, *Angela's Decision* would win its first film award and DP Aaron Gulley would win a Gold ACE Award from the Australian Cinematographers Society. Mat's skill at bringing the right people together and orchestrating it all would certainly not end with just a screening on my laptop. I would volunteer to enter the film in some festivals in the U.S., where it competed as a foreign film.

As the screenwriter, the only online submission site for festivals at that time, Without-a-Box (WAB), would not allow me to fill out the entries for festival submission. Mat gave me an additional title to screenwriter – I would become a co-producer. I would not be listed on the onscreen credits, but I would do much of the work of festival submissions and publicity, and later for distribution, as Mat, also one of the producers, and Kate Croser, the other producer, and the rest of the crew had pressing film projects waiting for them. *Angela's Decision* was a labor of love, and cast and crew had cleared their busy professional schedules to make this short film with Mat King.

Being a producer in post-production was on-the-job training for me. I really had no idea of how to determine which festivals to enter, not having experience or even thinking I would ever do this. I was just the screenwriter, after all. Once I had given the script to the director, then – poof – I was finished with my part. Go become a film.

However, my enthusiasm and desire to learn this end of film took over. I entered two festivals in Alabama first off, because, well, I was living there. We were accepted into one – the George Lindsey UNA Film Festival, which I had also covered for an Alabama magazine as a journalist in 2006. Then I chose festivals where I had lived before to give my entry some sort of a local connection (we'd moved fifteen times by then) or a film friend would refer me to festivals they had been to, such as the Tupelo Film Festival, the town known for being the birthplace of Elvis and only three hours from me.

I always had to be cognizant of festivals that were right for *Angela's Decision*, due to the length of fifty minutes. Most shorts are shorter than that, with a majority ranging from five to twenty minutes. In some festivals, the film was entered as a short, but in some it was entered as a feature. In some festivals, it qualified as neither. The film would go on to win awards in both categories, as a short and as a feature. We considered the Sundance Film Festival, but we would have to wait almost a year to enter for the following year, so we decided to forgo that festival and just get the film in as many festivals as soon as possible. I wasn't just a rogue festival submitter – I would consult Mat and get his approval. Again, the gold standard as a director. *Angela's Decision* was accepted into over half of the festivals entered, a good record considering the entries of hundreds, sometimes thousands, even in smaller festivals. (We'd also have to have DVDs made – now you can enter films online, saving that cost and mailing fees).

This film resonated with young folks, older folks, small town folks, city folks, and people in between. You will have to read the script and watch the film to understand why and come to your own conclusion about that. But more importantly, to me, Mat King captured why some young people are drawn to join the military, and the film made some people who were so positioned on both sides of for or against Iraq maybe think for a moment of those who are actually going to war, along with other issues in the film.

LESSONS LEARNED: As with anything in life, you'll experience some setbacks as I did with my first "Hollywood" deal (though grateful for the option). Around the corner, an even greater experience is waiting for you – if you're open to it. Never discount writing a short as just an exercise in writing. If you're not going to direct it, someone may be willing to take your script to a higher level like Mat King did with mine. If you can't be on-set as a writer, volunteer for other things in post, such as festival submissions, publicity, and distribution. That's what producers do. Become a producer.

ANGELA'S DECISION: Shooting Sample
First Two Pages
(photos and script courtesy of Mat King)

1 EXT. MONTAGE – SURROUNDING LANDSCAPE OF QUORN 1

July, Winter.

ANGELA JACOBS, 18, runs through an early morning desert landscape, which is back dropped by the Flinders Ranges Mountains. Angela runs and runs, approaching the deserted outskirt streets of Quorn, a small dying town in Central South Australia, 40kms from Port Augusta.

2 EXT. ANGELA'S HOUSE – QUORN – MORNING 2

A small, rundown house sits on the edge of Quorn. The front yard shows alternating patches of weeds and junk. The other houses on the street look the same.

3 INT. BEDROOM – ANGELA'S HOUSE – QUORN – MORNING 3

An old, beat-up dresser looks like a beautician's workstation gone wild, strewn with make-up, different size hairbrushes, curlers and a curling iron. In the clutter stands a high-school athletics TROPHY and some PICTURES of teenage friends.

A framed TAFE acceptance LETTER hangs on the wall, tilted. Blankets are thrown across a twin-size bed. Angela stands looking into the mirror, trying to pull her long, bleached blonde hair into a ponytail. She has a beauty beneath her too old-for-her-age fatigue. She sighs at her reflection.

A HORN HONKS outside.

ANGELA
Shit.

Angela grabs her blue K-Mart style work smock and puts it on. She stuffs some make-up, a brush and hair spray into her purse. She knocks over a PHOTO of herself and her boyfriend, WILL TURNER, then 16, in an Aussie Rules football uniform. She places it beside a recent PHOTO of Will in his Army uniform. Angela hurries.

4 INT. LIVING ROOM – ANGELA'S HOUSE – QUORN –
MORNING 4

Angela's mother, LINDA JACOBS, 37, sleeps in a chair, grasping a
cigarette in one hand. A water bong sits on the table next to her.

Still dressed from a night on the town at the local pub, Linda doesn't move
as the radio plays an old country tune.

Angela stands and stares at her, disappointed. We sense that this is routine
for Angela. She removes the cigarette and grinds it into a nearby ashtray.
She turns OFF the radio. She takes pity and covers Linda with a shabby
blanket.

The car horn honks again from outside. Linda wakes up startled and grabs
Angela's hand.

LINDA
What the hell are you doin'?

Angela pulls away, scared.

ANGELA
I'm going to work.

LINDA
You woke me up...

Angela throws the blanket at Linda.

LINDA (CONT'D)
...Well, I worked all night.

ANGELA
Yeah, work.

LINDA
Better than stackin' tampons all day.

Linda pulls some money out of her bra. Angela does not respond. She just
looks at her mother with disdain and disgust and turns to leave.

LINDA (CONT'D)
Now that Mr. Big Shot coming back to town today you're Miss High and
Mighty.

Angela does not want to listen and heads towards the door. Linda pulls
herself out of the chair.

(The film is available on Amazon. Photos courtesy of Mat King.)

RHIANNON OWEN
XAVIER SAMUEL

ANGELA'S
DECISION

Life is what you decide

PACE PICTURES presents a KING CROSER FILM "ANGELA'S DECISION" RHIANNON OWEN XAVIER SAMUEL
SOUND DESIGNER JOHN KASSAB HAIR & MAKEUP DESIGNER DEBORAH VAUGHAN COSTUME DESIGNER GIOVINA D'ANGELO PRODUCTION DESIGNER ALEX O'BRIEN
FILM EDITOR DALE ROBERTS MUSIC BY CHRISTOPHER SLASKI MUSIC & SONGS BY LIAM GERNER DIRECTOR OF PHOTOGRAPHY AARON GULLY
BASED ON THE SHORT STORY BILLY'S RETURN BY GENA ELLIS PRODUCED BY KATE CROSER & MAT KING
SCREENPLAY BY GENA ELLIS DIRECTED BY MAT KING

PacePictures
© 2008 Mat King. All Rights Reserved.

92

6 ON ATTENDING FILM FESTIVALS

I thought all three full-length narratives were well done, but I gave the nod to Angela's Decision *because of the impeccable performance by the actress who played Angela. She could be working in Hollywood right now, with no one to stop her. (She) reminded me of a young Meg Ryan - simply fantastic. Her performance is what true acting is all about.*

-Mark Thompson, Juror, George Lindsey UNA Film Festival 2007

The film festivals and resulting awards reflect greatly upon Mat King's expertise and vision as the director of *Angela's Decision.* I was able to go to a few festivals as the "filmmaker" who would field the questions at the end of the screenings – an amazing and a bit unsettling experience in itself for a writer who usually sits alone in a room with her characters. But this filmmaking process broke the norm in many areas. These are notes from just a few of the films festivals I attended. I recommend that writers attend at least one festival. Film festivals are for film fans, so go, even if you don't make films. You'll see amazing films, from shorts to features to animations to documentaries, that you may not find in theaters. While you may see them eventually on websites like Vimeo or YouTube, or even on Netflix or Amazon and the many other online outlets nowadays, there's nothing like going to a festival, seeing films in unique venues such as a vintage bowling alley or an old restored movie theater (much like the one I went to as a kid), and hearing the filmmakers discuss their films after viewing them.

George Lindsey UNA Film Festival (GLFF) 2007

I'd recognize that voice anywhere. That sweet Southern drawl that makes "bless your heart" sound like butter dripping off a biscuit into your mouth. The owner of that voice sits next to me and tells me how much she loved my film and that this is the third time she's watched it. She had been a judge. I'm speechless and I find it hard to concentrate on my own film viewing as she is one of my favorite actors from *Sling Blade* (the first indie film I saw in the 90s), and, in a film set in my home state, *October Sky* (also a film I had studied in my adaptation class at OU). But I feel like I'm sitting next to family and that calms me down.

I know I'll have to speak afterwards, and I have no idea what to say. Luckily the film students from the University of North Alabama, sponsor and home of the festival in Florence, ask questions, and one in particular practically stumbles over chairs to reach me as I leave the venue. Also, my script became a globally-made film and it was now returning to the American festivals – as a foreign film. How did that happen?

The audience applauds and I field some questions. Every festival I learn later on has a Q&A with the filmmakers present after their films are screened. I take a few questions from the mostly silent crowd. As I'm about to leave the room and take my poster down for the next film to screen, a student approaches me and asks me to sign his program. My first autograph!

"That's the kind of films that I want to make. How do I become that kind of filmmaker?"

I'm both stunned and honored by that question. How did I get to this point? After all, I'm not the prototypical, cool indie filmmaker – I'm a mom and Army wife living in Alabama, and I'm just that small town girl from WV who went to the movies every Friday night (though I do learn to wear some filmmaker black after showing up in my brighter-colored attire). Then what I have learned comes back to me, and I realize that he's talking about the kind of film that evokes emotions in people, makes them think about

94

the characters, their stories. He says he wants to be a writer/director.

He waits as I try to find some words of wisdom that will start him on his filmmaking path.

"Just write the stories you want to tell, that you want to see. Not what you think will sell, and you will make this kind of film." Hmmm, didn't I hear that from my professors? And it's true, it really is. I have proof now.

One girl seems to be giving me an odd look. Maybe she hates the film, maybe she hates the story, maybe she's been in that situation or knows someone who has been, or maybe she just wanted –

"I want to do this."

"What?"

"This, I want to make movies exactly like this. How do you do it?"

That is such a loaded question. It dawns on me that as the writer, yes, I did help create this movie. The festivals dub me a filmmaker just by being the one to represent the film there, so I start to call myself one too, eventually, though it feels a bit uncomfortable. One thing is for certain, a film begins with the written word. But how do I explain that this screenplay came from a bad short story, then I listed it on a website, and then it became a film in Australia with original music from Spain and London, with festival play in the US and abroad. It sounds so simple, so ordinary when I neatly tie it up like that. If Mat were here, he would probably know just what to say. He could also talk about the actual production of the film – questions I will steer away from. I almost feel like a fraud – I don't know cameras and lenses. (Until the film and Matt and others are featured in an Australian film magazine. Then I learn to speak camera, a little bit).

Then I realize that I can talk story, as a writer. I can talk about the story of how this film came about. How a writer from West Virginia wrote a story set there, then made it a script set in Oklahoma, and then how that became a film in Australia, with music made in the UK and Spain.

Adaptation. I can talk about that and write about it. I would eventually piece together press releases and give talks about the story behind the making of this story, this film, which intrigued folks as well as the film. The how it came to be (leading to this book to wrap it up).

So I simply say: "Write the story you want to see on screen and study scripts, not just films, really study the scripts of films you like." Ah, advice from my thesis chair. And write not just what you know, but what you want to see and read. Mantras of just about every writer.

Natalie Canerday. Linda in the Billy Bob Thornton film, *Sling Blade*, and Elsie in *October Sky*. That's that sweet, sweet voice beside me at my screening. And beside me later at lunch also. And she'd go on to help present an award to me later that night with actor Danny Vinson. *Angela's Decision* will receive her first award, in the feature film category – Honorable Mention (Second Place, tie) in Full-Length Narrative – our first festival and off to a great start. Many thought it was a full feature.

My name is called. I must make my way through the tables to get to the stage. The lights are hot and bright. Actor Danny Vinson hands me a certificate, but all I can focus on is Ernest Borgnine, from *The Poseidon Adventure*, seated right before me, clapping and smiling at me. Did he just give me a thumbs up? Oh, Marty, Marty. And George Lindsey also. (Who is Lindsey? Probably best known as Goober in *The Andy Griffith Show*, he has a lot of credits to his name that can be found on Imdb.com). I stumble through an acceptance speech and mention telling the stories of our soldiers. About getting it right. Their stories.

Who knew that we'd still be at war over a decade later? As I write this book a decade later since *Angela's Decision* was filmed, so many stories have been told by now. So many more to tell. For now, Angela's and Will's stories, and my own, take center stage at GLFF. I accept this award.

Garden State Film Festival March (GSFF) 2007

I'm surrounded by a group of young, but battle-hardened Marines. Not your typical festival screening experience. I'm about to go onstage with them after our films premiered at the Garden State Film Festival in Asbury Park, New Jersey. *Angela's Decision* premiered with their film in the block of Films About Iraq. Their film, *Between Iraq and a Hard Place*, deals with post-traumatic stress disorder after the battel of Fallujah. This is early in the war, even for talk about PTSD. It's March 2007. I think this is one of the first films about Iraq that I've seen, if not the first.

The Navy chaplain with them casts uncomfortable glances my way. I assume either he did not like my film or did not want me on stage with them. Maybe it was just the sex scene in my film that had made him uncomfortable. (It made me uncomfortable at that screening). Or perhaps he is uncomfortable around women in the military. I was, after all, a veteran, too, and had experienced that before. Either way, I feel, once again, like an outsider about to go on stage, just like I did at that Strawberry Festival years ago. I don't belong here with this group of Marines. They have done something very brave and suffered the true costs of war, of watching their buddies die. I also was not sure *Angela's Decision* should be listed with a film about Iraq just because it is mentioned briefly in my film. But then, on the other hand, this is exactly what I wanted – to show young people like these men on stage, making these tough life decisions. Their film showed the flip side of the decision – what can happen once you sign your life over to higher powers that make the decisions of war.

Then a couple of the Marines approach me. I have no gum to hide. No high heels, but I still feel a bit wobbly in the knees. They extend their hands to shake mine.

"Really liked the film."

"You did?"

"Never saw that ending coming. A total surprise."

"Really?" Words would not find me at that moment. I felt relieved and a bit like Sally Fields. They like me, they really, really like me. Or at least they liked the film and the ending was a surprise, and I had welcomed their response. The chaplain said nothing.

We would all go up on stage for Q&A. They were definitely the heroes of the hour. I kept my comments short. But when I talked about wanting to make a film that showed the "decision" being made to join the Army, what propels young people to join -- there seemed to be a recognition pass between us. The Marines and me. While the director of the film was not military, he did a great job of capturing the early fallout of this war. Later on, in the lobby, they would ask me to be in their group photo. I should have declined. But it felt like a reunion of sorts for me. Like I was a platoon leader all over again, an adopted one for a few minutes. However, I would never know what they'd been through except what I had seen on screen. That power of film thing again.

I was also in awe of the restoration of the historic Paramount Theater and took in some of the films in a multitude of venues, even entering Springsteen's Stone Pony. Seven years earlier my family and I had stood on the same boardwalk in a cold March rain and peeked through the door at the Boss giving a concert at the Paramount. It was a surreal feeling to go back to a place where my own short Army career had ended and think about the Kosovo refugees who had arrived in New Jersey from that war in 1999, to think about the impact of the 9-11 attacks and how the war in Afghanistan had faded away, and then to think about the invasion of Iraq in 2003 and how entrenched we still were in 2007.

This fest was a weird mixture of the art of film and the devastation of war, as I would watch the other films in that block about Iraq. I began to realize that that's what film festivals do. Not only could you see films you would not normally see in movie theaters or on televisions (back then anyway, much easier now online), but you could share in the experience of the actual filmmakers who often dedicated themselves to their film and to their subject matter, their cast and their crew, without monetary return. And just like with the young Marines, you may just get to meet the subjects of the documentaries.

Angela's Decision would be a finalist in Best Original Score for one of Christopher Slaski's tracts and would be in good company in the category of short films. James Gandolfini, who attended the festival, took that honor with his film, *Club Soda*. I ended up staying at the same hotel as the Iraq documentary director and *Club Soda*'s director. As a female Army veteran, I realized film was actually tougher for woman in some ways, as I would start to compare the two. I was also one of just a couple of female filmmakers there. I would notice that this would be a trend at the handful of festivals I would attend and realized that this was the norm – for festivals and for Hollywood-made films. Female directors or filmmakers were rare in attendance and screenwriters were even more rare, unless they directed the film as well. I was an anomaly on both counts. Just like in the Army, women were in the minority, only more so in film.

Most fellow filmmakers were silent about my film at the festival. Others asked stupid questions such as, "Do Army people cheat on each other when they go to war?" and "How can you trust your husband in the Army?" Questions no Army wife of then twenty-two years wanted to hear. Another gentler comment: "You don't look like you have a sixteen-year-old daughter, you look great for your age." My thoughts on those questions? What the hell did this have to do with *Angela's Decision* or with me as a filmmaker or writer? I am glad those types of questions did not surface at most festivals. Though I would notice the absence of women.

Tupelo Film Festival May 2007

If Mat King set the bar high, really high, for a great filmmaking experience for this writer, then Pat Rasberry, the Tupelo Film Festival director, set the bar high for my film festival experience. Tupelo became my third film festival (and I still have a relationship with the festival as a judge and workshop presenter). I will gladly grab any excuse to go back to this welcoming festival and town in Mississippi. (I'm writing a script set in MS and hope to film and produce it there). The festival volunteers are the best, along with the film-goers made up of the general public and the community college and high school student filmmakers. Their enthusiasm is unsurpassed. (I'll be going back to teach a workshop on adaptation at the local college also). Pat always brings the most interesting workshop presenters and filmmakers together in Tupelo (to include actors and musicians). This fest has given many a filmmaker a home and connections to other filmmakers. When I think of Tupelo, it's film that comes to my mind first, then Elvis second.

I am at the birthplace of Elvis, taking a tour of his old home. I have taken a break from the festival to get a picture of his home for my Mom. But I don't tarry too long. The schedule is jam-packed with films, events, and food, and I feel more at home here than I've felt almost anywhere else. My film is shown late on Friday night at the Lyric Theater. That's as it should be. The theater is almost a replica of the Groves Theater that I grew up with (minus the long stairway trek to the basement bathroom). My film is not for children, and showing it at night reminds me of sneaking up after bedtime, making the trek to the bathroom through the living room, to catch a peek at the ABC Sunday night dramas.

While I worried at first about screening my film in smaller festivals, I had nothing to worry about – the stories in my film pack a punch in a place like Mississippi. Small town West Virginia in *Billy's Return* was easily changed to small town Oklahoma and Australia in script and film version, and both could easily be interchanged with small town Mississippi.

A family of four that I'd been introduced to earlier approaches me; they are debating a storyline from my film upon leaving the theater. They want me to settle the debate. The dad and teenage daughter say Angela was pregnant in the film. The mom and other daughter say she wasn't. It just gave the illusion that she could be.

"Who is right?" they demand.

"Both. Both are right."

A point can be made for either outcome. While to some it does seem more likely in the film that Angela was pregnant, the film stuck to the script's intent to make it very hazy and lead people to draw their own conclusions. (I will hear this same argument again after screenings). Honestly, I go back and forth on it myself. Mat King has an opinion, but he kept the "choice" of both in the film. And that is exactly what I wanted. To be unclear. Not to mention this showcases the decision of joining the Army and two examples of what may lead up to that life-altering event.

Meeting other filmmakers at festivals is the icing on the cake, and Tupelo is no exception. I am being treated like a full-fledged filmmaker by Pat and her staff and volunteers.

I meet two filmmakers all the way from the former Yugoslavia – Montenegro, to be exact. I can only think of my small part in that wartime effort and ask questions about how the split-up country is doing, without offending anyone, I hope. I also meet a horror filmmaker from Virginia Tech and a documentary filmmaker from NYC (where my daughter will live and make films later on via Columbia University grad school).

One thing is for certain, if you attend festivals you'll meet people from all over the world, even at smaller festivals. No fest is too small.

It is awards night. I'm not feeling too well, but I go to the festivities and drink it all in, to include the soupy, humid air mixed with crepe myrtles. The awards are held in an antique car museum – dinner and dessert awaits. (I do not remember going hungry in Tupelo, ever). I take a Polaroid in my mind, as I know this will probably be the last festival I attend with *Angela's Decision*. As much as I want to go to Phoenix, I really can't afford another festival, and the Army wife life calls me back to reality again. Besides that, Mat is in the US and will go, as it should be. Luckily, Tupelo was only three hours away and I could drive, unlike the Garden State. And the fest picked up a night at the hotel. Again, smaller may be better. Enter and go.

As I sit next to a fellow filmmaker, Don Tingle also from Huntsville, at the banquet, I also meet a guest speaker from Oklahoma, very fitting as I tell him the story of the script. They announce the list of winners, and I'm glad someone I know is there to witness it. Another deserving film wins Best Short, the category that *Angela's Decision* is in, so I sit back and nibble dessert. I really do feel glad to be there. Then they announce the last award, the Ron Tibbett Best of Show award.

Wait. What did they just announce? I'm picking at my cheesecake, stunned. While I may have felt like Sally Field with the Marines at Garden State, I clearly have my Oscar moment at Tupelo.

Angela's Decision is awarded the top honor. Best of Show! I walk upfront to collect the handmade sculpture of a movie reel, along with a certificate and five hundred dollars. Small is very large, indeed.

Later at the after-party at a volunteer's home, I am congratulated by many and collect their business cards. Couple that with the Southern style dinners, sweet tea, and banana pudding – life is now complete. Time to return to Army life. Right? What else can you do with a short film that's feature-like, but not the right length to market to distributors? This is 2007. So I do not really give it a second thought – until later on.

Flying Monkey Arts Center, Huntsville, AL Premiere

Screen your film locally. That's what you do with a film of this length. With the help of my daughter, her friends, and my husband, we made our local premiere an event. Since *Angela's Decision* contained all original music, I contacted the local NPR station also. They not only played some of the film's music the day before our premiere at the up and coming Flying Monkey Arts Center, a local art venue, but they did an interview with me on-air and gave me a half-hour block on their weekday local programming schedule. Granted my film had a great slant – local writer makes film in Australia. Use what you have locally to draw folks to your screening. Made globally, seen locally.

We were accepted into more than half of the fests I entered. You will hear about top tier fests like Sundance, so enter them, but don't discount the small fests. GLFF would have the Sling Blade Reunion at their fest in 2008. I would be a film panelist and attend that year as well. Nothing like seeing Billy Bob Thornton play drums and banter with Natalie Canerday and Josh Lucas on stage. Not to mention meet Ernest Borgnine again! Natalie Canerday, Danny Vinson, and George Lindsey would become attached to one of my scripts. It was optioned but never produced. Others were on board, but it didn't make it into production before Lindsey and Borgnine passed away. And, as I mentioned before, I would develop an ongoing relationship with the Tupelo Film Festival that is still leading to new ventures, to include the publishing of this book and a research trip for another script and story.

LESSONS LEARNED: Attend festivals. Volunteer to write an article for the local newspaper about a film festival. Meet people. Make connections. Be nice. Be your own PR manager: if you don't love your own film, nobody else is going to do it. This is the icing on the cake (besides distribution), so eat all the icing that you possibly can. In film and in life, scrape the icing from the pan, too! And eat cheesecake – maybe your film will be announced best of show in mid-bite, too. Unlike the chewing gum at the berry festival, I didn't have to hide this. I have also included a sample press release for my film and a list of some awards. It's important to tell your own story of the making of the story. Promote your film. Promote yourself, in whatever you do in life. Somebody will want to know your story.

PRESS RELEASE AND AWARDS FOR *ANGELA'S DECISION*
Screenplay Becomes a Global Filmmaking Process

Even though set in Australia, *Angela's Decision* literally crosses many boundaries, both in story and in the filmmaking process itself. American writer Gena Ellis wrote the script as part of her graduate thesis at the University of Oklahoma in 2003 in just three days, before her husband deployed to Iraq. She listed it on InkTip.com. The script was adapted from her short story, *Billy's Return*.

The script was a Top 25 winner in *Filmmaker* magazine's American Gem screenwriting competition. Award-winning director Mat King found the script listed on InkTip.com. As well as directing, Mat King also produced the film, along with producer Kate Croser, also from Australia. The entire film was filmed and set in South Australia, with an Australian cast and crew, starring up-and-coming actors Rhiannon Owen and Xavier

Samuel, who will play Riley in the upcoming *Eclipse*, the third film in

104

the Twilight Saga.

Mat filmed the script in six days, with great support from the professional cast and crew. Gena was also made a co-producer and performed film publicity/marketing and festival submissions. Original music was written, produced, and scored in London, England by Liam Gerner and in Madrid, Spain by Christopher Slaski, a UK native -- both very seasoned musicians in many genres of music.

The Making of *Angela's Decision* was featured in *LipSynch* magazine in Adelaide, Australia. U.S. press coverage includes *Screentalk* magazine, the *Washington (D.C.) Times*, *Huntsville Times* (AL), *The Valley Planet* (AL), and the *Tri-City News* (NJ), and it was most recently mentioned in *MovieMaker* magazine. An interview and music clips from *Angela's Decision* aired on WLRH, an NPR station in Huntsville.

AWARDS 2006-2009

Gold Award, Best Cinematography, Australian Cinematographers Society

Karma Cup Series, Mercury Cinema, Adelaide, South Australia

Premiere, Flying Monkey Arts Center, Huntsville, AL

Honorable Mention (2nd Place tie), George Lindsey UNA Film Festival

Finalist, Best Film Score, Garden State Film Festival, Asbury Park, NJ

Best of World Cinema, Phoenix Film Festival

Best Adaptation, WorldFest-Houston International Film Festival

The Ron Tibbett 'Best of Show' Award, 2007 Tupelo Film Festival

View www.browndotproductions.com for a complete list.

7 ON BECOMING TV PILOT SCRIPT

It can be done – you <u>can</u> break into television writing. The industry is full of writers who somehow managed to buck the odds. Not all of these writers are related to somebody, nor did they all begin with contacts. Some of them lived outside of the LA area.

-Madeline DiMaggio

Some things do come full circle, and the stars seem to align in my favor once in a while. Strawberries are one of my favorite foods now, especially when drenched in chocolate or piled on a shortcake, and all those trips to the bathroom as a kid watching TV dramas would now come in handy again.

I am not standing on a stage – I am on the phone with my daughter, who is in college and interning with AMC – the cable network, not the multiplex chain. AMC Original Programming, to be specific. She's been tasked with finding a TV pilot wannabe script and taking it through the development process while interning there for the summer. Not only am I on the phone with her, but part of a teleconference with her boss, the executive assistant to the head of development for the entire network.

Angela's Decision has gone through yet another adaptation and has seen new life as a television pilot script, which was my original intent when writing the short script of TV drama length for my graduate thesis. This makes the <u>third</u> adaptation of the source material, short story *Billy's Return.*

The biggest full circle of all, though? My daughter, Ursula, giving me notes to make improvements on my original, adapted *Angela's Decision* script (not the script for the film, but the one I wrote in grad school). Real live development notes, complete with a deadline for a rewrite. Let me explain. She was sixteen when *Angela's Decision* finally became the Australian film, and after high school she went on to became a Radio, Television, Video, and Film (RTVF) major at Northwestern University in Evanston, Illinois. She had already written and directed grant-winning short films by the time she interned at AMC after her junior year.

Honestly, I was more nervous about being part of her internship than any stage time I had walked before, whether at pageants or at film festivals. You would think Mom might get special treatment, right?

Thankfully, no. Being her mother made no difference in that department. She had emailed me her notes earlier, and they were quite extensive – six pages worth. Notes are something that writers receive to make changes to their scripts. You hope that you write the perfect script, but that's usually never the case. I was on deadline at the most inopportune time – I was in the middle of our seventeenth army move (literally about to hit the road) to Chicago, and I was recovering from back surgery. I almost declined her offer to use my original script for her project. However, I managed to drive to Chicago, unpack my computer, and take many breaks while rewriting (and driving). She gave the script (and me) the kick in the pants that we needed. We both turned out better for the writing exercise.

Luckily I had already written a drama script for the TV show, *Brothers & Sisters*, on speculation for the ABC Disney Fellowship a couple of years earlier, so I knew the rhythm of writing the TV drama, not to mention how to place act breaks. That script was not chosen, but it was a great exercise in writing the hour-long script. Writing a spec script of an existing show, comedy or drama, or even your own pilot, offers you a chance to flex another writing muscle. You may write for old shows as well, but you will never be able to use that script except for practice. There are contests now where you may enter scripts of existing TV shows – not to mention, when you get an agent, you'll have an active calling card. (Plus the plethora of online venues such as Netflix, Amazon, Hulu, etc. that produce their own original shows now want pilots).

While most TV dramas always followed the four-act structure, ABC dramas switched to a six-act structure for *Brothers & Sisters* then, as they do now also (I just wrote one for *Nashville* on spec for the same fellowship). This allows for more ad revenue (and bathroom breaks, channel surfing, etc.). Regardless, screenwriting is still the same. Tell the best story you can, within the structure, format, and time limitations you have to work with.

Using the tried and true four-act TV drama structure, upon Ursula's recommendation, I condensed my original *Angela's Decision* script (the one in this book) into the first two acts, or the first half, of the pilot. I added some new characters and locations – Angela is only in her hometown for the first twenty minutes or so of the pilot. This involved deleting or combining some scenes and deleting characters, as well as, surprisingly, adding new ones. Coach Williams and her daughter, Randi, are new characters in the TV pilot script.

The second half of the TV drama now takes place during Angela's basic training time where Angela faces new challenges and has more decisions to make. I also took the story back to the original time period of the late 1980s – the film version was moved to 2006 (current day then).

The film, in essence, has now become what's called a proof-of-concept film, which allows *Angela's Decision* to become a TV series (this is also why I kept these rights to my script). The script and the film may stand alone, as the pilot differs enough from the film that they are both still separate entities. In a perfect world (and in the film *Boyhood*), I would have the same actors continue their stories throughout their military journeys for the TV series. Not the actors in the original film, though. The pilot script is still under consideration elsewhere, but I have included an excerpt. This is my full circle, thanks to my daughter.

LESSONS LEARNED: Have patience. Your dream, and your stories and scripts, may take different forms than originally intended so be ready and open for anything and everything. To include your own daughter giving you development notes one day. (Really, really extensive development notes.) And eat lots of strawberries. Because they are really, really good for you.

8 THE TV PILOT

ANGELA'S DECISION
"On a One Way Trip"

ACT ONE

FADE IN:

EXT. LAKE ROAD - RUNNING MONTAGE – MORNING

We see a female figure running on a road beside a wooded area on this crisp morning. A runner with steady strides, her breathing is smooth and even as we get closer. Breathing becomes slightly labored as she runs up a tree-lined hill. Leaves have turned and are starting to brown and drop.

The runner slows a bit as she crests the top of a hill, with the sun rising over a mountain lake that appears below. She hits her final strides, down the hill to a straight stretch towards her old 1971 Chevy Nova. It's 1984.

EXT. ANGELA'S HOUSE – DAY

A small rundown one-story house sits on the edge of Everly, a small dying town in West Virginia. The front yard alternates between patches of weeds and junk. A rusted car sits on cinder blocks. The other houses on the street look the same.

INT. ANGELA'S BEDROOM – DAY

An old, beat-up dresser looks like a beautician's work station gone wild – makeup, different size hairbrushes, curlers, and curling iron. A radio PLAYS .38 Special's "Back Where You Belong." In the clutter stands a track runner's TROPHY and some PHOTOS of teenage friends.

POSTERS of places like Germany and Hawaii adorn the walls. Pull outs from Tiger Beat magazine and a framed college acceptance LETTER from Calhoun Community College hangs tilted beside a 1984 CALENDAR from Nichols County Bank, full of tick marks, counting down the days until Oct. 28, which has a big heart on it. The Oct. 7 square on the calendar has letter P marked on it.

Blankets are strewn across a twin size bed in a twin size room, mixed with running clothes and worn out running shoes.

ANGELA JACOBS, 19, wears the small town dress code well — tight jeans, red sweater, and heels. She stands looking into the mirror, trying to pull her long, permed, bleached blonde hair into a ponytail.

She looks at her reflection and SIGHS, as she tucks her hair. Angela has a beauty beneath her too-old-for-her-age fatigue. A HORN HONKS outside.

ANGELA: Shit. Just a minute.

Angela grabs her BLUE WORK SMOCK (Wal-Mart-like) and puts it on. She grabs some makeup, a brush, and a can of hair spray, and stuffs them into her purse.

She knocks over a PHOTO of herself, in cheerleader's outfit, and her boyfriend, BILLY TURNER, then 16, in a football uniform. She places it beside a recent photo of Billy in his Army uniform. Angela grabs old tennis shoes and hurries out.

INT. KITCHEN/LIVING ROOM – DAY

LINDA JACOBS, Angela's mother, 36, talks on the phone, while smoking a cigarette, still dressed from what appears to be a night on the town at the local honky tonk. A RADIO PLAYS a Conway Twitty country song.

Liquor bottles line a counter. A frying pan with scrambled eggs smokes on the burner of the stove. A cigarette smolders in a nearby ashtray. Linda is too entranced in conversation to notice the burner or Angela. Linda laughs into the phone.

Angela stands and stares at Linda and her surroundings, disgusted. We sense this is routine for Angela.

Angela grabs the frying pan and slams it with a clatter into the sink, startling Linda.

Linda turns, waving at Angela, trying to grab the pan from Angela. The cord prevents her from reaching Angela. Angela runs water into the pan, making it sizzle, as Linda tries to hear the person on the phone.

LINDA: Damnit! Nothing. I'll call you back, Lou.

Linda slams the phone in the cradle. Angela braces for Linda's wrath as she grinds the cigarette into an ashtray.

LINDA: Hey, those are good eggs!

Angela's anger is taken out on the cigarette.

ANGELA: I don't want to call 9-1-1 so early in the morning.

Linda tries to grab her hand from the cigarette. Angela pulls away.

LINDA: Where you goin' so early?

Angela stands in the tiny living room in front of the VELVET ELVIS PICTURE. Knick knacks from Virginia Beach sit on a shelf.

ANGELA: I'm going to work.

Angela tries to straighten up the living room. A HORN HONKS outside again.

ANGELA: Which is more than I can say about you.

Linda dumps the eggs into the trash can, takes a long drag off cigarette, and opens the refrigerator.

LINDA: I worked all night. At the pool hall.

ANGELA: Yeah, work.

Linda cracks an egg into the watery frying pan and places it back on the stove.

LINDA: Better than stackin' tampons all day.

Linda rubs her head, then pulls some money out of her bra. Angela, disgusted, turns to leave. Linda counts out a couple of dollar bills.

LINDA: Here, take a couple of dollars for lunch.

Angela stops.

ANGELA: I don't need your money.

Linda laughs, grabs the handle of the pan, and stabs the eggs with a spatula.

LINDA: So, Mister Big Shot comes back to town today. And now you're Miss High and Mighty. Don't need my money, huh? You better watch yourself, Missy.

Angela, not wanting any lecture from her mother, rushes out the door.

EXT. ANGELA'S HOUSE – CONTINUOUS

Linda follows Angela to the doorway with the frying pan in hand. A car, rusted in spots, idles by the curb.

LINDA: Now that your cousin is gone, I don't need another mouth to feed around here. Especially one that takes a bottle.

Linda straightens up and waves to the car.

LINDA: Hey, Susan, nice to see ya.

Angela rushes to Susan's car.

INT. SUSAN'S CAR – DAY

Angela slams the passenger door shut. SUSAN RANDALL, 18, dressed in the same BLUE SMOCK underneath her coat, waves to Linda, then reaches back to check on one-year-old TOM JUNIOR, TJ as he's called, in his car seat.

SUSAN: It's okay, sweetie.

Susan places the pacifier in TJ's mouth. She checks herself in the rearview mirror, runs her hand through her short, brown hair, as Angela places her old tennis shoes on and throws her heels in the back.

SUSAN: I see your Mom is lookin' out for you again.

Angela sits, fuming.

ANGELA: Yeah, me and half the male population in Nichols County.

Angela watches Linda on the porch. Angela looks back at Susan.

ANGELA: Nice cut. Janice do it?

Susan nods and smiles, pulling the car out onto the road.

SUSAN: She is right about one thing. We don't need any more bottle feeders around here.

They look at each other and laugh, lightening the mood.

INT. VARIETY STORE – DAY

Angela arranges a rack of clothes in the lady's department. She picks up a PILLOW misplaced on the top of a rack and starts to take it back to houseware. But she stops in front of a full-length mirror instead.

Angela places the pillow under her smock. She poses and rubs her stomach, checking out her reflection. Susan turns the corner and drops an armful towels as she sees Angela. Angela smiles and looks at Susan.

ANGELA: How does this look on me, Ma'am?

Susan grabs the pillow and hits Angela with it. Susan places it under her own smock and pushes it to her chest instead.

SUSAN: Better fit up here, Ma'am.

Their uptight supervisor, MR. VINSON, 40S, sneaks up on them, holding a clipboard.

MR. VINSON: Miss Jacobs and Misses Randall, get back to work. Or someone else around here'll want a paycheck. With the mine ready to strike again.

Mr. Vinson marks something on his clipboard and WALKS OFF. Angela mimics him. Susan laughs, picks up the clothes she dropped and leaves.

Angela grabs the pillow and smoothes it out gently. She places it back underneath her smock for one more reflection.

EXT. PIZZA PARLOR – NIGHT

The parking lot is crowded. Music blares. This is THE place in Everly.

INT. PIZZA PARLOR – NIGHT

This hole-in-the-wall pizza and beer joint is busy. Angela stands near the bar, as Susan sits with TJ on her knee. She plays with a quarter in her hand. Music plays in background.

ANGELA: Okay, only one more quarter for the jukebox.

SUSAN: Yeah, I'm out. Fun, fun.

In the center of the room, tables have been pushed together to accommodate a large group of people. Empty pizza pans and pitchers of beer litter the tables. But the party has moved on to the POOL TABLE beside it.

A dozen or more GUYS, various ages, surround BILLY TURNER, 19, handsome

114

and well fit, sporting his class A dress uniform. He looks like an Army poster of the recruit that he is, being all that he can be. His JACKET drapes a chair.

TOM RANDALL, Susan's husband, and KEVIN SCOTT, both 19 and Billy's best friends, drink beer and shoot pool. Their main interest is hanging on to Billy's every word, as all are. Tom is unkempt and rowdy. Kevin is the steady, quieter one.

HANK, 15, an awkward teen, slows down while he's bussing tables to listen in. LAUGHTER.

Angela can't take her eyes off Billy. Billy nods at Angela from across the room. She raises her beer and takes a sip. Susan bounces Junior on her knee, as he gets fussy.

SUSAN: How much longer can they go on?

ANGELA: Guy time, then my time.

Angela looks at her watch.

SUSAN: Surely Billy is horny after bein' around nothing but guys for weeks.

Angela and Susan laugh. IMOGENE, 30s, pretty but tired waitress walks up behind them.

IMOGENE: Sure is a handsome one.

SUSAN: Thanks.

Imogene points to Billy. Angela looks his way.

IMOGENE: I was talking about hers over there, but he's pretty cute, too.

Imogene coos at the baby. Susan smiles.

IMOGENE: You ladies like a refill? On them?

ON BILLY. He laughs as he looks over at Angela, takes a sip of beer. Hank, trying to get closer, bumps Billy with his bus tray. Tom grabs his arm.

TOM: Hey, asshole! You know who you almost spilt that shit on?

The guys quiet down. Hank looks like he's going to crap his pants. Billy tries to calm the situation.

BILLY: Tom, it's okay.

115

Tom releases Hank.

HANK: Everybody knows who Billy Turner is, don't they?

Tom stares Hank down. Billy gets back to business.

BILLY: So, officers against enlisted, right. Drill Sergeant says, Turner, ever carry a football?

The guys laugh. Hank looks like he's witnessing the second coming of Christ.

KEVIN: Uh oh, here it comes.

TOM: Ever carry a football? Good one.

BILLY: Yeah. I said carried one all the way to state three years in a row.

The guys LAUGH. Tom gets agitated.

TOM: You should be at the university, Billy. Dumb asses.

Laughing subsides. Billy squirms a bit, sets up his shot.

BILLY: Army's gonna pay for college.

TOM: And the university can stick it up their ass. Taking away a scholarship for one bad grade.

Billy makes the final shot into the pocket. Susan, with TJ on her side, and Angela walk over to the guys. Susan pokes Tom in the arm. He gives her a look of death. Angela comes up behind Billy, gives him a hug. The guys say their good-byes.

YOUNG MAN #1: Party at the docks tomorrow night.

Billy leans back on pool table and pulls Angela towards him.

BILLY: May be busy for a while.

ANGELA: You damn well better be.

Tom starts to walk off as TJ cries louder.

TOM: I've gotta go take a leak.

Susan stops as TJ spits up on Billy's army JACKET.

TOM: Jesus fucking Christ, Susan.

SUSAN: Sorry. He needs to go home.

TOM: Nothin' stopping you from leavin.

Billy calms the situation again. Angela grabs the jacket.

BILLY: Tom, it's okay. Ang'll take it to the cleaners in Jefferson.

Angela pauses, then tries to wipe the jacket. Tom gives Susan a look and heads out. Susan gives Angela an exasperated look and follows Tom, her usual routine.

Angela holds onto Billy, as if he'll disappear.

BILLY: So, where you wanna go?

Billy turns full attention on Angela- finally.

ANGELA: I got paid today. Wanna get a room at the motel?

Billy downs the last of a beer. Gives Hank a nod, leaves a huge tip, and takes a good look around the place.

BILLY: What are we waiting for then?

INT. MOTEL ROOM – NIGHT

Typical cheap motel room, same tired look as the rest of the town. Billy and Angela stumble through the door, kissing, taking off their clothes, making way to bed. They stumble onto bed, ready for their rediscovery. Billy on top of Angela, kissing her. Billy wants more but pauses.

BILLY: You're still on the pill, right?

ANGELA: No, I told you it was making me sick. Hold on.

She fumbles through her bag and then dumps it on the bed, with Billy kissing her.

ANGELA: Here, use this.

Angela can't get the condom open. They laugh about their awkwardness and eagerness.

ANGELA: I'm glad you're back home, Billy. I've missed you.

Billy pauses and caresses her cheek. A tender moment.

BILLY: I've missed you, too, Ange, I've missed you, too.

And he really means it.

INT. ANGELA'S CAR – DAY

Angela sits in her HEAP OF A CAR at the only stoplight in town. A hardware store has a going out of business sign in the window. An ELDERLY COUPLE enters the store. The Pool Hall is further down the street.

Angela looks at her watch. She wears her old high school track suit. A pickup runs the red light. The light turns green. Angela drives on.

EXT. GAS STATION - DAY

A sweaty Angela pumps gas at a station across from funeral home. School bus drives past station. A very fit lady in a track suit almost like Angela's, COACH WILLIAMS, 30s, approaches her own car across from Angela.

COACH WILLIAMS: Some people think they can just keep school property and not get caught?

Angela turns about to say something not nice, then realizes it's Coach Williams, her high school track coach from last year. Angela smiles.

ANGELA: Coach, you know the office charged me for it last year. I just found it at the bottom of my closet last night. You goin' senile in your old age.

Coach Williams laughs. Angela grins from ear to ear. She's missed this coach-athlete banter.

COACH WILLIAMS: Oh, took you a year to clean your closet? Typical Jacobs. So how ya been? Haven't seen you in a while.

Angela places the pump back in the holder. Her smile fades away.

ANGELA: I've been working a lot.

COACH WILLIAMS: Heard you're going to community. That's great.

Angela's a bit ruffled.

118

ANGELA: Yeah. Couldn't go this semester.

An understanding passes between them.

COACH WILLIAMS: You'll get back there. Stop by sometime. I'm sure the gang would love to see you. And Randi, she always asks about her Angel.

ANGELA: I will, Coach. I will. Things have been... crazy.

Horn blasts.

COACH WILLIAMS: *(to husband in car)* In a minute. *(to Angela)* Anytime. You know that, Angela.

ANGELA: Thanks, Coach. I will.

Angela watches as Coach drives away, waving to her.

EXT. SHOPS IN JEFFERSON – DAY

Jefferson is booming compared to Everly. The SIGN says Medical Office, Dry Cleaner, Army and Navy Recruiting Stations, and a Beauty Shop. Angela walks down the strip, carrying Billy's JACKET, smiling, singing a happy tune.

EXT. DAIRY QUEEN – DAY

Angela pulls into parking lot.

INT. DAIRY QUEEN – DAY

Angela rushes into the restaurant to meet Billy, Susan, Tom, and TJ. She walks by TWO GIRLS, 17, trying to get Billy's attention. Angela bumps their table. They turn their attention back to eating ice cream and whispering.

TOM: Look, it's the lost smurf.

Angela slides into booth by Billy. He pulls her close and gives her a kiss.

Tom stuffs his face with a burger as Susan tries to feed TJ, who sits on her knee.

Angela reaches over and gives TJ a tickle.

ANGELA: How's my baby doin?

BILLY: I don't know about that one, but this one could use some attention.

Angela's more than happy to give Billy some attention.

TOM: Yeah, he's only got a couple more weeks.

Billy admonishes Tom with a glare. Angela turns to Billy, then to Tom.

ANGELA: What? Couple more weeks?

Angela looks at Susan for an answer. She shrugs.

ANGELA: I thought training was over.

Tom wipes his mouth and scoots Susan out of the booth, stuffing the baby food into the diaper bag.

TOM: We better go, Suze. Let these lovebirds do some catching up.

Tom grabs TJ and the bag, much to Susan's surprise. Susan starts to say something, but Angela's look to her says it all. She follows Tom out.

Billy puts his arm around Angela, as she slides out of the booth. She storms out of the restaurant, knocking the girls table again. Billy follows.

EXT. DAIRY QUEEN – DAY

Angela smacks a picnic table hard. Billy grabs her hand and tries to sooth her. She pushes him away.

ANGELA: What the hell, Billy? When were you gonna tell me all this?

MRS. TRENT, 50s, walks by and shudders at her language. Billy sits on top of the table, gives the lady a smile, as he pulls Angela onto the seat and rubs her shoulders. Angela tenses up, gripping the wooden seat with both hands.

BILLY: Hey, Miss Trent. Tell Smithy I'll be by this week.

MRS. TRENT: He'll be glad to see ya, Bill. Tell your Mom I still have her casserole dish.

BILLY: Will do.

Angela glares at all the goodwill. Mrs. Trent gives Angela the once over and goes inside. Billy slides down by Angela.

BILLY: I'm tellin you now, Ange.

ANGELA: Yeah, after Tom messed up.

Bill stutters around with explanation.

BILLY: My, my drill sergeant said I was a natural. Picked me to go active.

Angela groans and tries to stand up, but Billy pulls her back down. She's heard about the Golden Boy too many times. Angela stares straight ahead, so mad she can't look at Billy.

ANGELA: You said one year, then we'd get married. I've waited for you.

BILLY: I know, I know. But I'm going to Korea, Ange. I can make more money there and save it up... For us.

The news just keeps getting better. Angela runs her hands through hair.

ANGELA: Korea? Shit, Billy.

Billy pulls her closer, and digs in deeper.

BILLY: And you can get stuff real cheap there, Ange. How about some Nikes? You always wanted a pair. All the guys buy lots of shit there before coming back home.

Angela knows she's losing this battle.

BILLY: For their wives.

Angela clings to Billy and her desperation.

ANGELA: Well, I could go with you.

Billy laughs, oblivious to what Angela wants.

BILLY: No, I have to live in the barracks.

ANGELA: If we were married. Doug gets free housing for him and Mary.

Billy realizes he has to dig himself out now.

BILLY: Damn, Angela. Not in Korea. I can't afford both of us there.

Billy loosens his hold on Angela, who wipes a tear away.

ANGELA: I thought you said it was cheap there.

BILLY: Yeah, like Nikes and crap. Not living there. I'll get thirty days leave in May.

ANGELA: Leave? For where?

Billy chuckles at her lack of military knowledge.

BILLY: That's army talk for vacation days. It will be pretty then. You don't want an ugly November wedding now.

Angela straightens herself up, taking it all in. This seems to pacify her for the moment.

BILLY: Come on, let's get our favorite room. I'll splurge for a whole week.

Angela tries to process all this new information as she watches the Two Teen Girls leave the restaurant. Billy watches them, too. Angela gives him a push but he grabs her and holds on tight, as Angela sees plain old town of Everly in the background.

INT. MOTEL ROOM – NIGHT

Angela and Billy are making out on the bed. Angela is not enjoying it, at all. She's just going through the motions.

INT. ANGELA'S BEDROOM – DAY

Angela stuffs some clothes in a bag, then changes her calendar – to November. She grabs the photo of Billy and gives it a kiss, then heads out the door.

INT. PIZZA PARLOR – NIGHT

This night is pretty much the same. Billy sits with a group of GUYS, including Tom and Kevin. But he's not in uniform this time. He's wearing his high school letterman's jacket. Hank is now part of the inner circle.

BY THE JUKEBOX, Angela and Susan hang out, as Susan dangles TJ from her hip, glaring at the guys across the room. Angela makes a selection.

SUSAN: Damn him, asking you to wait again.

Angela still tries to reason this out.

ANGELA: He wants to save up –

SUSAN: I know. Save up some more money. Just how much goddamned money does it take to come back to this shit hole?

Susan voice starts to crack as she gets angrier.

SUSAN: Or get married? Hell, my wedding only cost fifteen dollars.

Angela is surprised as Susan thrusts TJ to her. Angela takes the baby as Susan RUNS OUT of the parlor. Angela meets Billy's gaze for a second, bouncing the baby on her hip now. Billy turns back to the guys. Angela walks

TO BILLY'S TABLE

Angela hands TJ to Billy, catching him off guard.

ANGELA: Just for a minute. It won't kill you.

Angela walks off. A very uncomfortable Billy hands TJ off to Tom, then rubs his hands on his pants like he just caught a disease.

EXT. PARKING LOT – NIGHT

Susan sits on the hood of her car, drinking a beer. Angela walks over and rubs Susan's arm.

SUSAN: Sorry, I'm just so tired.

Susan looks at Angela.

SUSAN: Do you really want to be part of the P-B-Twenty Club, Ange?

ANGELA: The P-what?

Susan jumps off the car, picks up some gravel, tosses one at her car.

SUSAN: Pregnant before twenty club. Yeah, you can join me...

Susan throws a rock for each name she calls out.

SUSAN: Janice, Christy, Tammy, Joanna...

Angela stops her and soothes her back to reality.

ANGELA: I thought Joanna went to WVU?

SUSAN: Did. A semester.

Susan straightens up.

ANGELA: Let me take TJ tonight.

SUSAN: No, you need to spend time with Billy. I'll take him to Mom's. At least I have her.

Angela turns away at the mention of a mother.

SUSAN: I'm sorry, Angela. I didn't –

ANGELA: I guess my Mom was a founding member of the club, huh?

Angela and Susan walk to the hillside by the Parlor sign. They sit down, with a good view of the Parlor.

ANGELA: Who in the hell came up with the B-P...

SUSAN: No, no, it's the P-B 20. Pregnant before. I came up with it. Hell, they have their club, why can't we? I'd like to be in man's world – for just a day.

Angela and Susan take some gravel and start hitting the Parlor sign.

ANGELA: Yeah, why can't we? Remember when our biggest decision was whether to use butter or baby oil for the best tan?

Susan laughs and downs her beer.

SUSAN: So you want to start the butter club or baby oil club?

Angela ponders this for a moment.

ANGELA: I'll take butter.

Susan throws another rock.

SUSAN: Guess I have no choice now.

END OF ACT ONE

9 ON BEING A (REAL) SCREENWRITER

You just have to keep on going. On that path. Sometimes it will be wide open full of everything you could possibly want. Sometimes it will be straight and narrow and you'll be impeded by others. Sometimes you might have to stop and change your shoes. Sometimes you'll have to take detours. Just be open. To what's along the way. On the detours especially. Just see where you end up. Throw away the map. And the GPS, too.

-Gena Taylor Ellis

Some women are naturals at walking in high heels, and some are just naturals on stage. I am neither. Still. This time I am not exactly on the stage, but beside it. And I'm wearing flats anyway. It doesn't really matter what I'm wearing, except to me. (I'm wearing a dress; I've worn like three in thirty years – I'm a skirt person). It's been over thirty years since I first stood on that stage at the WV Strawberry Festival. My screenplay is one of nine scripts selected for a Live Script Read at the Female Eye Film Festival in Toronto. The book I picked up at a flea market in Alabama? I finally adapted it into a screenplay nearly ten years ago, and after seven years of not being able to sit at computer (due to back surgery and residual effects), I picked that script back up again a couple of years ago and did some rewrites and placed it in competitions, again. It had placed in quarterfinals and semifinals in 2008. Once I rewrote it, it began placing higher during the past year – in the top four and as a finalist in every competition.

At FeFF 2016, the added bonus of being selected is not only the Live Read, but also the script development session of meetings with producers at the international film fest in Canada. I'm nervous. These are real actors, and

I know they know their stuff. As well as the audience and the seated judges before me. The book, *The Black Tulip*, by Alexandre Dumas, was written in the 1800s and set in the late 1600s. What I thought was relevant to 2006 was still relevant to today. When I rewrote the script last year, even though Rosa saved the day and the supposed "hero" and flower, she didn't appear in the book until quite late. So, trying to stay true to the book, in my adaptation she didn't appear in my script until the second act. And just like *Billy's Return*, even though I didn't write the source material of this script, it just bugged me. I realized that Rosa was the true hero of the story, and it was really her character that had the most growth, along with the tulip. So I moved her up and added some scenes. And renamed it *Rosa and The Black Tulip*. Then it all made sense. To me. But still. It wasn't a final draft of the script. I realized before I even went to the festival, after the lead actress who was to read Rosa's part contacted me about that part, that I needed to move her up even further from page 14, maybe even to page one or two.

I'm still a bit uncomfortable in large groups of women. While at the Strawberry Fest, they weren't quite accomplished yet, the women at the film fest were. Accomplished and inspiring to me. All of the films were directed by women. That was a new experience for me in itself. The screenwriters were all women (not a requirement), except for one male co-writer.

The films I'd watched so far were amazing. After going to fests nearly ten years ago with me being the only female writer or one of a handful of filmmakers there, to be at a fest that was for women and promoted them exclusively was overwhelming to say the least. Their topics were just as overwhelming. The film from Turkey that exposed the oppression of women with the surprise ending that gave both lead women power was very powerful to me and could easily be a film I'd see at a Landmark theater. The documentary about the rise of neo-Nazi power in Greece into the political arena there was scary and reminded me of my own military

126

endeavors to help save the world – that lieutenant in Germany who watched the Wall fall and the break-up of the former Yugoslavia (let alone my husband's 13 years at war, nearly half his 30-year career, well beyond my 12 years in the army). I cried. During both of them. Post Army life.

The biggest surprise waiting for me at the fest was reconnecting with a writer whom I had heard speak about her first published book in 1994 at the Antioch Writers Workshop – the same workshop where I took a screenwriting seminar and was advised by screenwriter Suzanne Clauser to take a different career path if I couldn't live in LA. Sharon Short, the novelist turned screenwriter, has seven novels under her belt now. And she gave me the sad news of Suzanne's passing earlier this year. She asked me to write a memorial piece for the AWW which was taking place a few weeks after the FeFF.

The Live Read went well. The actors, Ariana Marquis as Rosa, all did an excellent job. I had to answer some questions afterwards, and we also had a live critique. And I realized, as I was hearing my script play out before me while envisioning it in my mind, that I once again had stuffed the female lead too late into the script, just as in *Billy's Return*. The other writers and the judges advised me to bring her forward. Even page 14 isn't early enough.

I realized that it mirrored my own life in some ways. Rosa. Angela. We were waiting. Or we were assisting others. Putting them first. I had placed the male leads in greater positions. At first. I was also used to being in the background. My husband's career always come first. My family I made first. But now. Just as I had given Angela the spotlight ten years ago. And I had discovered recently that Rosa is the hero of the story, and I brought her forward, I realized, that at this point in my life, I needed to step out of the background and into my own life again. Army life was over, and family demands lessened. Now was the time to put both feet forward and step into the spotlight, onto that path (back pain, numb legs and all). Maybe that's why I was uncomfortable at FeFF at first (of course, the back pain was great from the travel and sitting through days of film). I was around women who demanded that they put their craft, themselves, forward. I wasn't used to doing that.

The story of Angela and Billy, unintentionally, paralleled our army and war journey in particular. The "official" combat operations in Iraq ended in 2011. I don't have to go into what's happened since then. All you have to do is listen to the news or read it online. Listen to the current political debates with the upcoming elections. I just add this book and *Angela's Decision* to the body of literature about the war in Iraq and let the readers and viewers decide and I hope for peace everywhere.

Our Army life is now over. After 30 years of Army life and half of it at war, well, there are scars. There are problems that need addressed and veterans that need help, as do marriages and children that make it through all that with their own war wounds. Nobody I know is unscathed, but there is help. My catharsis is writing (and maybe one day I'll write a true memoir). My own daughter has added to that body of work about Iraq with her poignant film, *War Is Kind*, her 2012 senior film project at Northwestern, which her dad and I were able to work on with her and her amazing cast and crew. (Only the second time I'd see him tear up about his own war experience, as it's also been placed in a compartment).

I no longer write romantic comedies in the tradition of the guy saves the girl. And there's nothing wrong with that story line. I still love Tom Cruise's line "you complete me," in *Jerry Maguire* (I used that script and film when I taught screenplay analysis at Webster University in St. Louis). And Meg Ryan, what's not to love? But my stories grew as I did. We both adapted. There's romance/comedy in my script-in-progress about a farmer in Mississippi. And there's romance in my thriller/mystery set in West Virginia. But I'm tackling some tougher subjects and my female leads are front and center – just like Angela and Rosa. The decline of the coal industry. Sex trafficking. The farmer in Mississippi who is gay.

Later, at the awards at FeFF, my name will be displayed on screen when awards are given out. Best Reserve Screenplay. I'm not sure what that means (I'm later told it's runner up). But after watching the film that won Best of Show, *SPLit*, by Deborah Kampmeier, which encapsulates so much about being a woman, I'm honored to share my award alongside these women. I don't remember everything I say when I accept the award. I do refer to film festivals I attended nine years ago and how I was one of few women there. I thanked those who helped make my script better. Three directors ask me afterwards for my script. Including the director of the Best of Show (I'm rewriting the first 15 pages now and sending it soon).

I walk back to my hotel alone. The street, Queen Street, is lively at night, so I'm not worried being alone. I'm staying at the LGBT pride headquarters for Toronto and it's a week after the nightclub shooting in Orlando. Confidence and sorrow in the same cocoon. I have spoken with a few that work at the hotel. I tell an employee there about my script that I'm working on now. He had given me a birthday slice of cake the night before when he found out I was there on my birthday, alone. I think of him. The festival ladies I've met. Leslie-Ann Coles who founded and has run the festival for 14 years. Lindsey Connell, the script development officer, who guided us through the process. My neighbor's daughter in St. Louis accepted into a film program. Pat, the Tupelo fest director and now good friend, who is fighting for her life but ran this year's festival in spite of that. And I think of my daughter. Who is pursuing her dream. I think of scouting locations in my home state of West Virginia where Ursula will film later this year. How she won a 20k grant from the Alfred P. Sloan Foundation and a quarterfinalist in the Nicholls Fellowship – all by the age of 25. At her age, I wanted to be a writer, but instead I was standing in combat boots, pregnant

129

with her in Germany, watching a country struggle to reunite, and later worrying about my husband who might deploy for the first Gulf War. And Angela. I think of Angela and the women now in the army. We all have stories to tell. Many stories.

Do I have any regrets? Maybe I'd change the pain. I still want to go to LA one day. But no. No regrets. These experiences, including the pain, made me the writer, the person, I am. However, I realize what Suzanne Clauser was telling me 22 years ago in Yellow Springs, Ohio. Instead of Lessons Learned, I'll close with the write up for AWW for her memorial. And I realize how funny life is, and you just never know where you're going to end up. A pageant girl, wannabe writer stashing gum under her dress, then wearing combat boots and jumping out of airplanes, eventually writing a film made in Australia, and now standing next to wonderful women directors and writers in Canada. My advice? Be open. To change. Adapt. And keep on going. Try something new. A novel is my undiscovered (and unfinished) frontier of writing. Maybe a blog. Definitely another script.

It's Friday night in St. Louis. I'm off to go watch *Forrest Gump*, on the outdoor screen at Art Hill in Forest Park. Some things never change.

A Thank You from One Script Girl to Another

In Memoriam

Last year, as my husband and I were driving through Dayton, Ohio, after his 30-year army career had finally given way to retirement, I thought about Suzanne Clauser. When I wrote my book about my journey of becoming a screenwriter, I had to give her a mention in the first chapter. I had wanted to be a screenwriter since I was in my teens and announced it on stage during the West Virginia Strawberry Festival Pageant in the 80s. When film program choices were either east coast or west coast and unattainable for a small town girl from West Virginia. There was no Internet to even look up screenwriting or film programs. So I became an army officer and then a freelance journalist.

Fast forward twelve years later to 1994, after I'd left active duty, due to injury and becoming a mom, and a move to Dayton area via my husband's army career and after I'd taken a short story class at Wright State University. I discovered the mother lode of writing -- the Antioch Writers Workshop. Not only was John Jakes the featured speaker, but there was a joint screenwriting-playwriting panel, featuring a woman screenwriter at that. I'd long had a fascination with not only wanting to learn screenwriting, but with books to films- adaptation- and how that came to be. Suzanne Clauser had not only written for *Bonanza* (a rarity for a woman), but she'd also adapted a John Jakes novel and her own novel, *A Girl Named Sooner*. Not only was she the first screenwriter I'd meet, but Antioch was my first writing conference. I approached this lady who was no holds barred on the panel. She seemed a tough broad who told you the way it really was- or was going to be. I asked her one question -- how do I become a screenwriter if I can't live in LA. Straight up, she told me to try another career path. So I did. I went home and started a novel. And one chapter in, that became my first screenplay. I just had to write a script. A few. As an Army wife and a fairly new mom, I knew I'd not be living in L.A., so I had to find my own door to screenwriting. And I did. But I'd eventually know what Suzanne meant. Film was a tough business and being outside the headquarters of it all would be a strike against me. Even as a screenwriter.

I found a way. And meeting Suzanne at Antioch was my first step. I'd think about Ms. Clauser again when I pursued my graduate degree in screenwriting at the University of Oklahoma and graduate in 2003. I studied adaptation and also read a book called *Script Girls*. A book about women screenwriters who led the way since the beginning of film. Suzanne was a script girl. Though I'm not sure she'd like that term. As someone who started out in a mostly male world in the army and transitioned to film, I could relate to Suzanne and I'd come to understand Suzanne and what she was really telling me. She was just trying to weed out the ones without the drive and determination to pursue screenwriting. The ones not cut out for being a script girl. She was telling me it was going to be tough, there were no givens, no matter where I pursued screenwriting, even if in the heart of LA or out in the cornfields of Ohio. With options in LA (without ever stepping one foot there) and a film made in Australian (a script I adapted from my own short story), several writing awards, and even becoming a producer and an actor on screen, I'd like to think Suzanne would be proud. Or at least give me a credit. A film credit. For not giving up. For becoming a "script girl" and still one, 22 years later, thanks to her and to AWW.

Christmas Tradition
(based on Korean War letters home)

Every Christmas Eve they know to leave her alone. To herself, to her thoughts, and to her box. Since December 1952, she'd established this tradition, and she'd only changed it once, ten years later. But that addition was also written in stone now, just like the Macy's Thanksgiving Day parade happened year after year. This was the only day of the year she allowed herself to succumb to remembrance, grief, and resurrection, all in one sitting. She reaches into the top of her hall closet with trembling hands and retrieves a box. It could be the emotion or it could be the Parkinson's finally setting in.

Daisy Fields makes her way to the kitchen. The kitchen hasn't changed much either through the years, except for a few updated appliances. The copper kettle clock. The yellow linoleum that shows wear and tear, but still holds hidden footprints of secrets and memories. The porcelain cookie jar in the shape of a stove, full of soft sugar cookies – Archway brand. This time of year the sprinkles are green and red. The grandkids will sneak them out of the jar and nibble on them in the shadows, and she won't be far behind, sweeping them up all over the house, though not as quickly as she used to. A routine she looks forward to each year.

The same drawer holds many time-worn recipes. Peanut butter fudge will be the chosen one for this holiday. And in the day of timer-ready coffee makers, she still clings to the percolator coffee pot, stainless steel because it makes a better cup of coffee than those automatic drip ones. She has a Mr. Coffeemaker in the top of her closet. A Christmas present from one of her daughters-in-law. She will set it out whenever they arrive from Alabama, and then put it back in the box after they've gone before New Year's Day.

The aluminum ladle at the sink to get a drink of fresh well water still hangs on its rung by the sink. No use getting a glass every time you just need a sip. Hepatitis and other diseases are of no concern to her. She raised these people, they breathe the same air. One good sneeze will spread just as many germs as sipping from the same cup, she determined long ago. She has no dishwasher, other than her own two hands. They offered to buy one a long time ago. Jelly jars in the window with starts of plants, trying to give them life. Blackberry jam jars – his favorite. All of the same memories float in the air each year, like smells from the kitchen stove to the non-living room.

The dinette holds the same arrangement it has held for years. A real butter dish with real butter, a honey jar with a wooden spoon, a silver tray inserted with crystal salt and pepper shakers with a carrying ring. A lone molasses jar completes the set. She wonders if anyone even eats molasses anymore. He used to love it, pouring it over his homemade biscuits and soaking up the dark liquid with the tokens from a mother who didn't have conveniences. That's what they call them now. Convenience, something she never made fuss over.

The red and white checkered table cloth displays proudly with small nicks in it from a lifetime of children and grandkids. It has faded to pink in spots where the sun hits it in the afternoon. Maybe she will get a new one for Christmas. It can sit in the closet with the Mr. Coffeemaker, taking up needed space, along with a never-used electric blanket.

The kitchen counter is worn from years of kneading breads, preparing meals and pounding meats. A glass jar sits next to a wire bill collector. Round pink candies beckon hands small enough to reach in. Peppermints. A drugstore on Main still sells the old-fashioned candies because they know she is a valued customer, what with all of the prescriptions she has filled there for the year. The store is a dying breed, though. Old man Harvey still keeps it open for the old-timers who feel Wal-Mart is too much for them. He doesn't need the money, so he refuses to sell. Her kitchen is an indication that everything can become significant, if you give it a place in your heart and memories.

She takes her place at the kitchen table, carrying the shoe box, like she was carrying the weight of the world and the Queen of England's crown at the same time. She sits the box on the table with a thud, revealing the pain of its weight. She gently unties the worn string with hands trembling, like she's opening a greatly anticipated Christmas present. Nothing fancy. But she had never been fancy, she had been practical. She caresses the box, like you would a child with a scraped knee, removing the lid with care because the sides are worn with age. A heavy sigh, like a release of a thousand balloons, escapes from her tiny frame.

She retrieves two Christmas candles from the counter and places them on the table in crystal holders that matches the salt and pepper shakers. Her hands tremble as she lights the candles with the old style metal lighter. She'll need to replace it soon. She bought a whole decade's worth from Sipens variety store before they went out of business.

She stares into the box. At first glance, it looks like most other boxes full of memories – old letters, assorted keepsakes. You could smell the dust of a country in struggle escaping, a time that most have never thought of since. The dust mixes with the lingering Christmas scents from a day's worth of baking – cinnamon, vanilla, and pine from the living room. Why did they call that room the living room when she seemed to do most of her living in the kitchen? It was his favorite room. He loved to eat.

She inhales as she takes out the contents. She places the first stack of neatly bound letters on the table. Red ribbon, his favorite color. The military stationary gives away the first clue that these aren't just ordinary letters. The red, white, and blue alternating trim on the envelopes reminds

135

her of the old barbershop poles. He used to get his hair cut at Sam's on the corner of Main and Vine. An old leather billfold, an official government letter, and other remnants of his life stay on the bottom. She will get to that in due time.

She unties the ribbon and the stack of letters stand at attention before her. Not a single one falls to the side, as if they've been expecting her. She takes a letter out of the first envelope and puts her spectacles on. That's what she calls them. The dark-rimmed glasses are actually in style now. She saw a teenager with pink hair wearing them at Wal-Mart the other day.

She'll read them in the order received. The first letter takes her back to Jerry's basic training. He's being brave, but he's homesick. He misses her biscuits and asks if she could *please send some homemade fudge*. He can receive it as long as he shares with everyone. She smiles. It's written haphazardly, as though he was in a hurry and lacked of sleep. He's been on guard duty, walking his legs off for four hours, 10 p.m. to 2 a.m. He says it will get better after he gets out of basic. He's in Texas and it's hot in April and he hates the storms. He says to tell Nimrod, his baby brother, that he wishes he were here, *it gets lonesome. Write a lot* – a direct order to her.

His other letters from Basic are about the same – the heat, the storms, and the lack of girls – which makes her laugh. *Tell Nimrod to be good, ol Hoppy, too, and Patty Cakes hello and to stay away from the boys.* Big brother always looking out for his sister. Patricia hated when he called her that once she got to high school. He asks about the garden, whether they've built the porches yet, or gotten on the city water line. This takes her back to a time in her life that erases the lines of age and worry. That's part of why she reads his letters. It's not just him; it brings back such a happy, sweeter time in all of their lives. He doesn't have his assignment yet. She remembers she had wished he'd get stationed somewhere on the East coast, maybe that air force base in Dayton, Ohio, so he could come home on the weekends.

One of his letters talks about a big plane wreck at Lowry AFB, Colorado, where he was receiving his follow-on training after basic. *Eight boys were killed in a training accident.* Who said war was the only thing to worry about? He says the plane had crashed into five homes off the base, and *it was a hell of a mess.* Her stomach tightens. She still remembers the fear she had for him before he left. There was a war going on in Korea, but nothing like the war before it. You didn't hear much about Korea in the paper, bits and pieces, but not much about any great battles. Not in 1952. They had been in talks that year for peace, though they were still drafting into the Army. That's why he joined the Air Force. Her first-born son, off to a war in a land nobody cared much about, or could even point to on a map. Lordy, that was 50 years ago now.

His October letters remind her of that draft. They'd called up some 30 thousand of them, *getting ready for the big one*, he writes. Like Normandy, everyone around these parts had figured. He talked of that and of the upcoming presidential election. Ike had run on the promise to end the Korean War, and that had tugged at the heart strings of those mothers and fathers like her who had a son there. It also tugged at those mothers who had had husbands, brothers or others killed or maimed in the last war. Those smart politicians. That had been one way to take the talk off the miners' troubles that year. They didn't want unions, those big coal companies, just more money in their pockets from the backs of her people. Her husband had been a miner, and her father, and it seemed like everyone else's. That was destiny in this part of West Virginia. Her son had wanted to see something different. Yes, a smart strategy to get a vote, talk of ending war. Nowadays everyone seems to want war. Her generation, though, knows the later wars had never brought the body bags home like the Great One. She hoped they never would.

Those were the golden years after the Great War, yes indeed. The vets had come back and started back to school to learn a trade or go to college under the GI Bill. Even gave the country tract housing. Suburbs, they call it now. Her town, though, was too small to have that. They still lived in the same house, depending on the same vein of coal, whether the strikes or layoffs would come or not.

She has to focus again and picks up the birthday card he'd sent to her in September 1952. Ringed with rows of daisies and a loving expression, it was signed simply, *love your son*. He was a writer of few words, but that made each one all the more meaningful to her. She'd sent him a birthday card in October for his nineteenth birthday. Probably too juvenile, with toy trucks on the front, for a grown man, but she didn't have a store devoted to cards like they do nowadays. She places the card back in the envelope.

The percolator culminates in a fury of finished coffee, bringing her to reality for a minute. She gets up from the table and pours herself a cup, adding two teaspoons of sugar and some cream. Real cream. They don't like for her to drink it now, but at her age she doesn't figure one jolt of caffeine will send her into cardiac arrest. Losing her son didn't kill her, at least all of her. This is part of her annual ritual, she drinks it the way she'd taught him to drink it. She used to sneak it to him at the age of six after he'd knocked out his first tooth. His father said he was high-strung enough. Better to get him hooked on coffee instead of the bottle, she'd argued. She'd always protected him. The coffee didn't ease the pain, but it made her senses heighten enough to get her through the letters, and the memories.

Her own grandchildren paid three dollars for one of these coffee concoctions at a fancy coffee shop. She turns up the old dial radio fixed on the local station playing Christmas music. They had bought her a digital radio, but it was at the top of the closet, under the electric blanket. The music will help get her through the Thanksgiving letter and onto December. He writes more and more about coming home in six months.

138

One year is all he can stand of this place, Korea. He wonders if all the leaves are off the trees back home and says *there aren't hardly any trees on the mountains over here at all.* He calls them Bald Mountains. There is a Bald Knob in West Virginia, and he doesn't want to see it when he gets home. He reminisces about a family trip up to the top and how Nimrod puked his guts out on the way up because of the curvy road. She misses those roads, curving so much that you could look down and see the cars on their way up behind you, like a snake uncoiling. Now they literally move mountains to make a road, or a coal mine. He asks about the mining fire he read about in the hometown paper that his sister sends to him, and when would Papa Time, a nickname for his father, go back to work.

He had so many worries there, but he was always concerned for those back home. Of course, he couldn't talk too much about the work he was doing or where he was located. She'd suspected somewhere near the front line, but not actually on it like in the Army. Another reason for him to join the Air Force, at least he told her that to feel better. He tried to help the family and would always send his checks home, keeping only a few dollars for himself.

He writes about all of his friends getting married back home. *I might like that too.* She smiles. He'd started up a romance with a girl back home on his last time to take leave. He needs someone to think about over there and look forward to coming home to. He'd always sworn off marriage, but war always brought out the need to love someone in men, have someone waiting back home. Or, was it the need to procreate in the wake of all that destruction, she wonders. Did that girl ever think about him over the years? She doesn't linger on those thoughts too long. It is too painful to think about what could have been. She concentrates on what was, instead.

She is jittery now from the coffee and sugar, and her hands shake as she takes the last letter. Yes, her senses are heightened now. She holds it in her hands, as if memorizing it through touch like reading Braille. Just like she had memorized his face before he left. A little crook in the nose from missing a fly ball. She still sees him as a boy, a young man, in her mind. What would he look like now? She pushes those thoughts aside.

He asks for more socks, said *it is getting cold as hell over here at night.* Nothing monumental, nothing to say to warn her. She had looked for signs in this last letter when it arrived two days after her notification from the War Department. Some recognition that he would have known, seen it coming, perhaps could have prevented his final outcome. But there were none. Instead, she looked for comfort in his final words.

Wish I could be home for Christmas but it will be just another day for me, a day of work. Tell Hoppy, Nimrod and Patty Cakes to rip into the presents real easy. Love your son.

Nothing to say, Mom, I'm going to load a bomb on a plane tonight and, while doing that, it will explode. I won't survive, and I won't get a purple heart, because I wasn't in combat. I was just doing my job. She's even lost her bitterness towards the War Department, as it was called back then. What does a medal mean now? It won't bring them back. Accident or not, it is a wound that still runs deep for her, and a purple heart will not give her a new one.

She rubs his signature – *love your son.* The words are fading away from this annual tradition. She inhales deeply again, as if it will bring him to her somehow. And it does for a moment in her mind, the dust from Korea, the Christmas smells. Cinnamon, vanilla, pine.

She checks the bottom of the box and knows what is waiting for her. The yellowed newspaper article jumps out at her. The headline reads, *Two Die in Korea. This Christmas will bring no 'peace on earth and good will' to two Nicholas county families who, this week, were informed by the War Department that their sons died in Korea.* This headline used to send her into sobs, but she remains as quiet as newly fallen snow.

She picks up the government letter. The Air Force had determined that his life was worth 650 dollars and 22 cents. That is what the *DD Form 397-1, Public Voucher For Six Months of Gratuity Pay* stated. Gratuity? Six months' amount of his monthly base pay. Did they think that's how long it would take to get over the grief? Why not seven? That finalized it for the military. She didn't recall the young man who had delivered the news personally. They told her she had blacked out, and he had left before she came to. Maybe there really was a Santa. Only he delivered something unwelcome that year.

The leather billfold was slightly charred from the explosion, but it had survived. It had been a Christmas present from her the year before. She goes over its contents. A coupon in it reads, *3d Bomb Wing, Airman's Open Mess, Good for 1 Beer.* Maybe that was his one thing to look forward to all week long, a free beer. A copy of the Air Force's *General Orders* is in a side pocket. This had instructed him on how to be a good airman. A few money order receipts from the money he sent home. His motor vehicle license from the state of West Virginia. He'd been saving up for a car.

She takes out his copy of the *New Testament Bible*, given out to all soldiers and airman. He had signed the back statement that indicated he had accepted Christ as his Saviour on June 3, 1951. That was before he'd even seen Korea. A card sized copy of the military's phonetic alphabet sat in the Bible, marking *Hebrews, Chapter 11.* She had kept the marker there, as if not wanting to disturb the word of God between him and her son. Maybe he was studying that verse, in particular *Hebrews 11:8-16.* The guidance page in the front of the hand-sized bible recommended those verses when looking to find help when Leaving Home. She was glad he had had Divine guidance. That's how she explained it, anyway. And it made her feel better.

His ID bracelet, the silver stretch kind so popular back then, engraved with his name had also survived. He had been wearing it that day. A gift from the girlfriend. She had called in the beginning and stopped by. But she had to go on, married and raised a family. It had survived unscathed. The Air Force soap holder and an address book with the names of his fellow airmen are all that remain in the box. She had received cards from some of them, but they weren't in this box. This was his box and his alone.

"Have a holly, jolly Christmas," sings the radio. She wonders how long she has been at this. She checks the clock on the wall, as if she is waiting for more. No tears fall. This is just a tribute to his memory now. Just like putting up the Christmas tree, baking the applesauce cake, and going to church at midnight. She places the items and letters back into the box in the order she took them out. She laces the string around it.

It is about time. Time for the others to come home. Time to put the box in the closet and get out the coffeemaker and electric blanket. She walks the box back to its place of glory. The newsbreak from the radio follows down the hall. *Talks between North and South Korea have resumed and this time there is hope.* A shadow follows her down the hallway, and the candles flicker. She smiles. She's grown used to the shadows and doesn't fear living alone now. Her son, a man of few words, but words with so much meaning would say *it's about damn time.* She shuffles back to the table and takes a bite of an Archway sugar cookie after dipping it in her last bit of coffee. She waits.

A knock at the door shakes her back to reality. She glides to the door with a worn smile on her face. Mr. Kim, who used to deliver her Christmas ham, enters with his middle-aged daughter.

When he took over the corner grocery store ten years after her Jerry died, he had worked hard to be accepted and delivered the hams himself. But since super stores and old age crept in, his daughter just delivers him now, along with a Hickory Farms ham, to Daisy's doorstep every Christmas

Eve. Right on the dot at 6 p.m. She'd never thought about what the Koreans had lost at that frozen moment on a December day long ago. Other than that country had taken her son, and her along with him at times. Mr. Kim had lost two sons and a wife in that same year that took Jerry. And a country was still divided. Oh sure, her neighbors and family had huffed and hawed about it at first. Some never spoke to her again. But she let Mr. Kim make this change to her Christmas tradition.

Daisy shuffles to a cabinet and removes a tiny teacup, sitting behind the spices. She and Mr. Kim will sit at the faded, checkered table cloth and drink something stronger than coffee and watch the shadows on the wall. And smell the dust of kindred spirits, and cinnamon, vanilla, and pine, as remnants lay scattered across the table of a past with no boundaries.

An Ethnography of Those Left Behind, circa 2004

Jump-jump-jump-
Over the sea; what wonderful wonders
We shall see!
Jump-jump-jump
Jump far away;
And all come home
Some other day.

- Kate Greenaway, from "Little Girls Jumping" Picture Poems,
Newson Readers - Book One: Good Times, 1927

Taking a look through the ViewMaster of war, her images are jumbled in no particular order, like a DeLillo novel. But if you dissect her mind, you will be surprised by the images in the jar, turning in the formaldehyde; there is a pattern if you know what to look for. Now, everyone, "Prepare to look," a drill sergeant echoes in the background as the caissons go rolling along.

She unpacks her books and magazines for what may be their final Army move from Oklahoma to Alabama. No sir, no Rocky Mountain high for her. Twenty years of memories in a cardboard castle, exhuming the Over There tour, complete with bronze star, four-leaf clovers (from before he left) taped to index card, photos of sandstorms and camels, silver necklace with her name written in Arabic, receipts and lists. All intermingled with her issues of *Vanity Fair.* Army movers don't discriminate, nor do they recognize sanctuaries.

The December 2001 issue with Brad Pitt on the cover catches her fancy. Brad's walking out of the ocean, pants soaked and abs and chest expertly exposed – dubbed the All-American heart throb. Cover reads: "He bucks up our spirits by making two big films, keeping Jennifer happy, and showing us his abs."

144

Another headline advertises an inside minute-by-minute account of United Flight 93. And if that's not enough to make her feel better, there's a special report on Bin Laden and germ warfare. She's had this post-9/11 dream before, mixing it with Iraq, but not a good fit in her sandcastle dreams.

She flips through the magazine and comes across the captioned Flashback photo, "Fanfair: Window on the War, Wounded Soldiers of WWII watch Victory Parade as it passes Halloran Hospital, 711 5th Ave on June 12, 1946, photo from The Daily News." Where will they be in 55 years? Mr. President, she would like an answer.

Some memories do not fit so neatly into a single viewing. She must come back again.

A psychic's note falls to the floor – anything with 3 will be bad. So she skips ahead to 2004. In that bookstore, Howard Dean is on the cover of *Rolling Stone*, and Wes Clark is the cover guy for *The (Gay) Advocate*, Jessica Lynch is squeezed in with books at a thirty percent discount, along with Hillary, Bush, and Clinton. The Left eye, the Right eye, and Princess Di. Everything in order, embedded reporters on the Telly. Wills, power of attorney, school lunch to prepare.

She takes a shower in the humidity of her new home. His face is embedded in her mirror like the Virgin Mary, the Hero of our Time, He is. In thy Mercy hear me. Quick, call CNN, and tell them He is here. She believes in Shinseki, sand dollars and steam – the three golden rules. They hold vigils outside her house – senators come to pontificate and the crowd gathers for a public hanging of yellow ribbons. Her daughter's friend is an artist and they sell T-shirts for $9.11, along with lemonade and pretzels with mustard, but not French's, only American-made, like ketchup. Red, blood red, that's the only way. Her other friend films it on the Victrola.

She auctions this mirrored miracle on EBay to the highest bidder and gives the money to the young soldier's wife. You know the one, who gets by on food stamps while sending new boots to the big sandbox. Army-issue ones hurt his feet, don't stand up well in the heat after the first 1,000 miles. Thank God for Uncle Danner boots in 11 wide, only $236. All the comfort He needs. Maybe they will sell good knockoffs at Payless for the others.

A mirage of Bill and Senate Bills, with free desert postage for Army families, provides an oasis for CEOs skinny dipping into their retirement funds in Barbados and Colorado. They do support the environment, the 22,000 square feet kind. She spots a leopard and dips her pretzel in ketchup, while He drinks from the cool aid.

The teachers of her youth were right – she would need math some fine day. They did not teach her geography in school, though, as she unrolls the map and flushes the toilet.

She reinvents herself a mechanic and will send the tools of war in a 72-inch box. Length plus width plus girth. The coffee pot is too big, so she goes postal, and they relent because He can't make it to Baghdad without it. There are so many uncertainties in war. W+L+G = 72 is a known unknown of the underfunded.

After coffee, she uncovers a receipt from War, the early years: a Sangean 14 Band AM/FM Digital WorldBand Radio, a Photo Smart 620xI Digital Camera, and 2.1MP RES 3X/4X Zoom 8MB Memory. Connections to the Truth. Arifijan is 25 degrees 54' North and 48 degrees 11' East if she needs to make travel arrangements. One jump per mile is 7,000 times.

Another note. Handwriting specialist says she dreams too much – she shouldn't have curved her T so much. And that she loves Eastern European cultures. That could explain her own camouflaged dreams about the little village girl of Kosovo. Soldier girl, remember when she said: *You look tired, ma'am. Here, take my apple from the Red Cross wagon, please.*

She is fading, like the sands of time through the looking glass. *The*

Officer's Wives Handbook (1956) says to stay busy in times like these, no gossip mongers allowed. She walks on the treadmill at 4.5 miles an hour as she chews on two Bazooka Joes. She collects five million gum wrappers for the fortunes and the jokes and turns up U2 with Bloody Sunday and A Beautiful Day looped. Did you hear the one about the scud rooms, which are two doors down and look like septic tanks? She runs with Him while Three Doors Down plays Here Without You. She turns the cardboard disk and laughs.

They were right, Hell is hot. She needs water. She drains the steam from the mirror and empties the tears from her pillow and ships them over in a rustproof container to the civilian making 15. K. He'll know what to do.

The lists and receipts are too many and too senseless:

On March 13, 2003, $90.30 for a phone call to Kuwait at 11:23 p.m.

HIS: Ranger Joe's International in Columbus: Deet, 2 oz. pump, piece of carrot cake, T-shirt from Airborne school, travel mug, chocolate, suntan lotion, markers, and brass padlocks. HERS: PX, Oklahoma: mailing tape, static cling flags, bubble wrap, toilet seat covers, travel baby wipes, macadamia nuts, toilet paper, peanuts, magazine touting Jackson the good father.

Pick him up at the Regional Airport at 12:25.

There's the Georgia O'Keefe poster of *Patio Number IX* bought on road trip to New Mexico with daughter. Daughter writes about monkeys in the White House while Napoleon leads the tour of the Abiquiu. She steps through the green door to bring him back. But it only works in movies. War Is certainly Kind in 2012. She closes the lid on Talk Radio, Moore DVDs, and the box.

She now sits in a house surrounded by boxy homes and boxy neighbors on red clay. They peel the Kerry stickers from her mini-van and throw bagels at her from afar. She watches the foreign people spray weapons of mass destruction on every weed in their green, green grass, all from their shiny, black Hummers. Her house swims in weeds, navigating the brackish waters of Southern living.

She takes the Sherman Alexies and William March's *Company K* and places them beside the bag of Steinbecks. She shakes sand out of the bag that holds her daughter's beach towel. The one stomped on by the thieving, duck-kicking Lutheran girls at the Lake in Oklahoma.

She closes the *Vanity Fair* and shuts the stereoscopic dream. All for the low, low price of one billion dollars a day. When He returns they will retire in Hawaii with the General and talk about the good old days of Kosovo. And she will watch Him walk out of the water, and She will squeeze the salt from His wounds and unbutton his desert camouflage shirt. Then they will pose for the Flashback photo for *Vanity Fair*, December 2056. He'll wear his $236 boots and all, in 3D. While bucking up our spirits...she'll step into Strawberry Fields forever.

For J.

Never The End

ABOUT THE AUTHOR

Gena Taylor Ellis is a daughter of Appalachia where storytelling is as old as the hills. She is a writer, and a journalist, an army veteran, a producer, and a background actor on TV shows, such as *Chicago Fire* and *Nashville*. The background of life is where the best stories are mined, so Gena can be found there, digging up stories for her scripts, her blog, and even a novel in progress, plus giving seminars and workshops. Gena is from no-woman's land by the lake town of Summersville, WV. A Canvas Grade School alum, she is also a graduate of Marshall University and the University of Oklahoma. View her website at browndotproductions.com and her latest venture at genaingeneral.com. View LinkedIn for official business-y stuff.

54296809R00086

Made in the USA
Lexington, KY
09 August 2016